LETTERBOX

OTHER TITLES FROM BLACK BEACON BOOKS

Novels by Cameron Trost:

Flicker
Letterbox
The Tunnel Runner

Collections by Cameron Trost:

Oscar Tremont, Investigator of the Strange and Inexplicable
The Animal Inside
Hoffman's Creeper and Other Disturbing Tales

Anthologies:

Samhain Screams
The Black Beacon Books of Mystery
The Black Beacon Book of Ghosts
The Black Beacon Book of Horror
The Black Beacon Book of Pirates
Steampunk Sleuths
Tales from the Ruins
A Hint of Hitchcock
Murder and Machinery
Shelter from the Storm
Lighthouses
Subtropical Suspense

blackbeaconbooks.com

LETTERBOX

Cameron Trost

BLACK
BEACON
B O O K S

Letterbox
Published by Black Beacon Books
Cover design by Cameron Trost
Copyright © Black Beacon Books, 2021

Black Beacon Books
blackbeaconbooks.com

ISBN: 978-0-9923211-4-7

Cameron Trost is an author of mystery, suspense, horror, and post-apocalyptic fiction best known for his puzzles featuring Oscar Tremont, Investigator of the Strange and Inexplicable. He has written four novels, *Dead on the Dolmen, Flicker, Letterbox*, and *The Tunnel Runner*, and three collections, *Oscar Tremont, Investigator of the Strange and Inexplicable, Hoffman's Creeper and Other Disturbing Tales*, and *The Animal Inside*. He runs the independent press, Black Beacon Books, and is a member of the Australian Crime Writers Association and The Short Mystery Fiction Society. Originally from Brisbane, Australia, Cameron lives with his wife and two sons near Guérande in southern Brittany, between the rugged coast and treacherous marshland.

camerontrost.com

1

Ian Carew lived directly opposite Mary Hopkins, whose garden was undoubtedly the finest in Mirebury. It was the first thing he saw as he left his house each morning. Even with winter blowing its chill breath across the moors, smothering the flowerbeds in the churchyard and the village green, her garden remained resplendent, oblivious to the change of season. Every once in a while, Ian ventured to ask what her secret was, and she would rattle off the names of certain plants and summarise her techniques, pleased as punch to share her knowledge. The key was to plant and fertilise the right varieties at precisely the right time to ensure yearlong greenery. It was rather like conducting an orchestra. While the musicians in one section were keeping quiet, waiting for their cue, those in another were trumpeting away. But unlike an orchestra, with brass, strings, woodwind, and percussion instruments kept apart, her garden was a patchwork of deciduous, semi-evergreen, and evergreen plants harmoniously intermingled. She offered Ian advice on just how to tend to a garden's every need, so he could try his hand. But all that took too much effort to follow, and at any rate, he was too busy marking homework or catching up with friends at the pub to spend time on his own disgraceful front yard.

Mary was also a force of nature in the kitchen. She baked the most delicious cakes and biscuits, apple and rhubarb pies, and cherry tartlets, using ingredients from her own garden whenever possible. She sold them at the Mirebury market every Saturday. One morning, a man had appeared at her stall to buy some of her delicacies. She remembered he was tall and of solid build, with wild red hair speckled with strands of grey. His baggy green overalls had hung from broad shoulders, and at his big-booted feet, a fox terrier had waited impatiently, sniffing in the direction of Jack Fuller's sausage stall. As a stranger to town, he'd stood out like a sore thumb and drawn the attention of the local gossips. Mrs Hopkins had asked the stranger where he came from and he'd replied that he lived in a village about forty miles away. He'd heard about her remarkable cakes and come all the way to Mirebury just to try them.

She would never forget that day.

As far as she could remember, the chap never came back, and the townsfolk found that rather strange. It was unthinkable that anyone could taste her baked delights and not like them. She could only conclude something terrible had happened, preventing him from making the trip back to Mirebury.

Ian closed the front door and headed down to the gate.

'Good morning, Mrs Hopkins.'

She looked up, straightening her back as best she could, and waved at him with a hand full of freshly uprooted weeds.

'Ian, my boy. How are you?'

'Very well, and yourself?'

'I can't complain. You're ready for another day at school?'

'I certainly hope so. Someone has to teach those young rascals a thing or two.'

'Make sure you keep them in line, won't you? I know they're harder to handle these days than when I was a little darling, but that's all the more reason to make them pull their socks up. Mirebury's future is in their hands.'

Ian smiled indulgingly. She told him the same thing almost every day, the wording varying ever so slightly, but he acted as though it was the first time she'd given him the keep-them-in-line speech.

'Don't worry about that, Mrs Hopkins. I promise you they aren't as mischievous as the class I had when I was teaching in London. You wouldn't believe what they get up to in the city.'

She nodded thoughtfully as she dropped the handful of weeds into a bucket. London was on the other side of the planet as far as she was concerned.

As Ian turned back to close the wrought-iron gate behind him, he whispered to himself, *'So, have you found a lovely young lady yet?'*

'Oh, Ian,' she called out in a voice that was hushed but still loud enough that any passers-by would have easily heard. Ian let out a subtle sigh.

'You haven't met a lady friend then?'

Ian smiled at her and shook his head.

'Not yet, Mrs Hopkins, but you'll let me know if you have any candidates.'

In truth, he was tired of her constant enquiries, regardless of how well-meaning she was. It was bad enough going to bed alone night after night without being reminded of his celibacy the moment he left the house in the morning as well. He wanted to find someone, to share his life with a *lady friend*, as Mary so quaintly put it, but the pickings were rare in a small town like Mirebury. Of course, there had been the odd intimate encounter in the six years he'd been there, but nothing that had lasted. Every time he got close to a woman, a problem would worm its way into the romance. In the first year of his life in Mirebury, one charming woman, Hayley, had been obliged to leave Mirebury for work reasons just a few days after they had met, so they hadn't allowed themselves to become too attached. Another, an ambitious artist, just hadn't been his type, far from it in fact, he'd suspected she needed psychiatric attention and made the mistake of sharing his thoughts with her. The ensuing heated argument had signalled the end of their short but passionate relationship. She had since left Mirebury.

So, day after day, Ian went to school and came home to an empty house. Like most single men, he went to the local pub once or twice during the week and ate out with colleagues and friends, but that couldn't stop him from feeling lonely, especially when most of his acquaintances were already married. Mirebury was a typical moorland village and its inhabitants followed a traditional lifestyle. Rare were those who weren't married with children by the end of their twenties. Ian was considered strange on account of his being over thirty and still single, but the townsfolk dismissed this strangeness as going hand in hand with being from the city.

'If only you were a few years younger, Mrs Hopkins,' Ian told her. 'You're a truly wonderful woman.'

'You know they don't make women like me these days, Ian.'

'That's so true, and what a shame it is.' He shook his head. 'Have a lovely day.'

The school was an easy five-minute walk from Ian's house. In fact, just about everything in Mirebury was at most a five-minute walk from everything else. That explained why there was almost no traffic in the sleepy streets of the town. Now and then, a delivery vehicle would pass by or a farmer would drive into town to do his banking or shopping, but otherwise the townsfolk got around on foot. The only bus that came into town at that time of the morning was the school bus. The secondary school students and some workers caught a coach that left at roughly a quarter to eight and headed towards the bigger rural centres.

Ian passed the church, located in the heart of town, and admired its stone bell tower caught in the morning sunshine. It was often hidden in a heavy blanket of fog at this time of the year, and on foggy Sunday mornings, only the peal of its bells would betray its presence.

In front of the church, the village green occupied a small area. It was slightly elevated and irregular in shape, like a triangle with the most acute angle hacked off, and there was a short stretch on the lowest side where small stones embedded in the earth formed a retaining wall. On this side, the furthest from the church, there was a decommissioned red telephone box now used as a street library and occasionally given as a meeting point for locals welcoming friends from out-of-town. Near the highest point of the green, closer to the church, there stood a Celtic cross war memorial. The carved stone monument reminded the townsfolk that a number of residents had known tumultuous times, a far cry from the mundane and predictable existence the others had always taken for granted. The Mirebury village green also accommodated two ancient oaks, a disused water pump with smooth stone basin, and two park benches where residents would sit and read, smoke, or appreciate the flowers in spring.

Opposite the telephone box were all of the most important

institutions, mostly housed in unassuming two-storey stone buildings with battered slate roofs. There was the town hall and the police post, the latter being little more than an office adjoining the former, as well as the local bank branch, the post office, the grocery shop, the bakery, and one of Mirebury's few restaurants. Only the bakery was already open at that time of the morning.

Ian liked to arrive at school with plenty of time to spare so he could drink a couple of mugs of coffee and run the day's lessons through his head before the first bell. He and Liz were generally the only ones who took advantage of the common room in the morning. The headmaster only came to see them before class if he had urgent news.

'Morning, Liz. How are you today?'

'Bloody tired, Ian. Do you know what it's like to be a mother?' said asked him, almost accusingly.

'I don't even know what it's like to be a father,' he admitted.

Liz taught the youngest children, from four to seven years of age. Teaching four-year-olds and teaching seven-year-olds were two completely different jobs, but since there were no more than nine or ten children within that age bracket, the classes were combined. She managed very well, according to the headmaster. According to Liz, she just barely kept her sanity. Her mother looked after her young daughter while she worked and Liz picked her up on the way home. She was surrounded by children all day long. Her only escape was in her sleep, and there wasn't much of that.

'Here you are,' she said, handing Ian a mug of strong coffee.

'Thanks.'

'You know there's a new librarian coming to town, don't you?' She looked at him teasingly over the rim of her coffee mug. If she'd been smiling any more broadly, her coffee would have leaked out of the corners of her mouth and flowed onto her immaculate white blouse.

'No, I didn't actually. Why the funny look?'

She swallowed her mouthful of coffee and laughed. It was a charming laugh issued from between equally charming lips, thin but soft in appearance, and always ready to wear a caring smile or playful smirk. Her eyes were the kind that could be hazel, golden, or green depending on the light, framed by crow's feet and faint bags. She was a beaming girl and an exhausted mother in the same body, and every inch of her humbly declared her devotion and goodwill for her family and friends, students and colleagues, and neighbours. Liz was the kind of woman who was wooed and wedded barely out of her teens in towns like Mirebury.

'The funny look is because I've been told she is young, pretty, and likes reading.'

'How very strange that is. I can't imagine a librarian who likes books.'

'Fair point, Ian. You got me there. But you've managed to conveniently skip over the key details; young and pretty.'

Ian sipped thoughtfully at his coffee.

'When does she arrive in town?'

'There you go.' A grin as wide as the moors. 'I knew you'd be interested. I don't know when she gets here, but I'll look into it for you.'

'I didn't say I'm interested. I haven't even seen her yet. But I'm not opposed to you keeping me informed. Just do it discreetly this time.'

She gasped in mock offence.

'When have I ever been indiscreet?'

'Need I refresh your memory?'

'No,' she answered quietly, pretending to be ashamed.

Ian drained his mug and checked the common room clock to see how much longer they had before class. There was easily enough time for another coffee.

'You win, Liz. I've taken the bait. Tell me, what else do you know about this new librarian?'

She eagerly raised the coffee pot and he held his mug out to accept a refill.

2

Mrs Hopkins washed her hands and slipped out of her gardening shoes before going back into the house. Every day at that time of the morning, except when she had other pressing engagements, she prepared herself a cup of Earl Grey and attacked a crossword. The daily rituals in life were important to the widow. Both her simple pleasures and her self-imposed duties gave her a sense of contentment and order. They provided her with a framework. She spent the earliest hours after sunrise working in her garden, weeding, planting, or pruning as required, then she did a crossword and drank her tea with a cloud of Brett Greyson's creamy milk. She would read the newspaper and sometimes write to a friend, and she always paid a visit to her husband's grave.

She finished her cup of tea and sat staring at the crossword puzzle. It was more difficult than usual. She would have to get Ian to help. He was clever with words and always happy to lend a hand. *At the sharp end of fashion?* Fourth letter *l* and sixth *t. A beast of venery?* Third letter *r.* It was no good. She pushed the paper aside, got up, and put her coat on.

The walk to the cemetery was a short one and traced a route she knew intimately. She knew every detail of every house in her street and could name its occupants, most of whom had been there for many years. In a town where after six years one was still considered a newcomer, as was Ian's case, it wasn't difficult to know just about everybody, especially when they considered you to be like a grandmother to them.

She passed through the cemetery's time-worn gateway, feeling at ease within the stone walls of the town's resting place. It was her husband's home, and although he couldn't speak to her or hold her in his arms, she could speak to him and keep him informed about what was happening in her life. It was calm, as always, in the cemetery. She was the only regular visitor in town. It wasn't that others didn't miss their dearly departed, just that they communed and contemplated in more internalised ways. She was used to being alone with Mirebury's former residents.

She tightened her handwoven scarf around her neck and crossed her arms over her chest. It was growing colder by the day, and anyway, when she was at her husband's resting place, she felt the cold more intensely. She remembered the nights when they had held each other to stay warm, and it was only since his death that she realised she'd taken those moments for granted. She would have loved to be in his arms again, instead of staring at a block of faceless stone.

'Good morning, dear,' she whispered at the name engraved into the headstone. She imagined the way he would have replied if he'd been able, the way he used to reply, how he used to smile at her and call her *honey*.

Without a doubt, Mr Hopkins's grave was the best decorated and the most meticulously maintained in Mirebury. Most of the others were flowerless, and many, even worse as far as Mrs Hopkins was concerned, still bore the rotting stems from Mothers' or Fathers' Day. Very few of the deceased were fortunate enough to have fresh flowers every week.

She stared at the flowers she'd placed on the grave two days earlier. They were still full of colour and the petals were strong and holding on. She smiled to herself. Her garden really was a feat of horticulture.

A crow flew overhead and landed in a skeletal tree. It cawed, disturbing the otherwise complete silence that hung over the sacred ground. Trees surrounded the cemetery, on the far side of the ancient stone wall covered in moss and lichen, and there were often crows in those trees. They watched everything that moved within the cemetery, which outside of Mary Hopkins's visits was limited mostly to the comings and goings of a few stray cats and field mice. They cawed at Mrs Hopkins when she came to see her husband, and she felt, as ridiculous as the idea was, that they were mocking her. For this reason, she disliked them. Sometimes she arrived at the cemetery and found one too close for comfort to her husband's grave, and she would chase it away with violent gestures and hissing sounds that belied her tender nature. She understood why her pagan ancestors had considered that particular bird to be a messenger of death. There was something undeniably discomforting about the crow; perhaps the sound of its call and the way it stared intensely, ravenously awaiting death. Ravenous, after all, was that bird's adjective, and one that never failed to make her pause a moment when she encountered it in a crossword puzzle.

'I'm going to see Gerald today,' she told her husband. 'He's doing well. His health is really quite all right. You know he walks an hour every day now, since the doctor told him to? He has even cut back on the whisky.' She laughed. 'Amazing, isn't it? Gerald, of all people.'

Mary turned around and tightened her scarf again, she'd felt a sudden chill, but not because of a draught of air. There was no wind whatsoever. She couldn't quite put her finger on it. The notion seemed a strange one to admit to herself, but she'd always trusted her intuition, and it had always served her well. She felt as though she was being watched.

She looked around the cemetery. It was a forest of cold stone, and there wasn't a movement. Nothing disturbed the stillness around her. The only other living creature in sight was the crow.

'Damned bird,' she whispered to herself, and then turned back to her husband. 'What was I saying, dear? Oh, yes, Gerald. Well, he's going to Portsmouth in a few days to see an exhibition on naval weaponry. That sounds fabulous. There'll be all kinds of arms from canons and cutlasses to torpedoes and guided missiles. I'm sure he would have liked to do that with you, just like the old days.'

She sighed and looked about again, but perfect stillness pervaded.

'Just like the old days,' she echoed herself nostalgically.

The crow cawed, and there was a haunting fade at the end of the note it held, as though it too longed.

Mary Hopkins stood in silence for a moment before saying goodbye to her husband. She had some shopping to do, then lunch with Gerald. Later in the day, she would read for a while before baking a few biscuits to share with her friends and neighbours when they dropped in to see her.

She believed it was best to keep busy. That was how one prevented dark thoughts from settling in the mind.

She blew the headstone a kiss before leaving.

3

After school, Ian walked to Jack Fuller's butcher shop. His friend was still working when he arrived, busy preparing a dinner order for Mayor Larkins. It was a generous meat tray consisting of traditional and spiced pork and lamb sausages, pork and cider sausages, rump steaks, tenderloins, and beef and bacon rissoles. Most of the butcher's work was done in advance because he knew who wanted what and when the customer would come to pick the order up. Even when his regulars didn't place an order, he usually had a good idea of who was likely to come on any given day. For this reason, Jack's display shelves tended to be rather empty and gave the false impression that business was quiet. In reality, he spent more time in the preparation room adjoining the shop than behind the counter.

'Jack! You've got a customer!' Ian called from the entrance.

A chubby face with red cheeks appeared through the PVC strip curtain hanging in the doorway.

'Sorry, but I've closed for today.'

The face disappeared.

'Jack! That's no way to welcome your favourite customer.'

The face popped back into view.

'Favourite customer?' He laughed, his cheeks lighting up like neon signs.

'What's that supposed to mean?' Ian asked with a look of feigned surprise.

'It means that although you're my best mate, you're far from being my favourite customer. I sometimes wonder whether you're a *vegetarian*, or one of those *vegans*.' He practically spat those two words out as though he had a bad taste in his mouth.

On Jack's list of the world's most despicable types of people, vegetarians were ranked as being worse than politicians and only slightly more socially acceptable than "those crazy American lads you hear about on the evening news who get dumped by their girlfriends once the latter realise they're antisocial nutcases and then go and shoot their classmates dead during an algebra lesson before blowing their malfunctioning brains out all over the baseball diamond".

'It's just because I only buy for one,' Ian pointed out. 'Everyone else over the age of seventeen around here has a wife and kids.'

'Point taken,' Jack said, rubbing his face with a large gloved hand. 'All right then. You can come in.'

'Thanks, Jack.'

'But first, could you give the sign a little twist?'

'With pleasure.'

Ian stepped back to the door, looked to see that nobody was approaching, then turned the sign so that CLOSED was facing the street.

'Come back here.'

Jack's voice was typical of a butcher. The deep tone and steady rhythm inspired confidence that the man knew his meats; precisely which part of which animal each cut comes from, and how to prepare any cut to mouth-watering perfection. It was impossible not to obey.

'I've got something for you to try.'

Ian liked the sound of that. It meant his taste buds were about to be treated to a delicious sample of Jack's expertise. The butcher was also a talented chef and somewhat of an amateur culinary historian. Knowing that Ian was a man of history as well, he never missed an opportunity to chat to him about what Henry VIII's favourite dishes had been or how Napoleon Bonaparte had revolutionised his empire's cuisine in his downtime between bloody battles. Ian and Jack would often sit together with a plate of succulent meat and a bottle of red and talk for hours about the world in general or Mirebury and its inhabitants in particular.

But that night, they were going to dine with Jack's family.

Ian stepped behind the counter, parted the strip curtain, and slipped into the back room.

The solid butcher was dressed in a blue and white apron, held a nasty looking knife in his gloved right hand, and wore a blade-resistant mesh glove on his left hand. In front of him was the meat tray he'd been preparing.

'That looks great, Jack. A real feast fit for a king,' Ian commented.

Jack smiled at the compliment. 'I don't know about a king, but it's as good as old Larkins deserves.'

The butcher nodded towards a sealed container sitting on a rack at the end of his work bench.

'Try a bit of that. It's cold now, but you'll get the idea.'

Ian lifted the lid off the container a removed a cube of the cooked meat inside.

'It smells delicious.'

'Go on. Stick it in your gob.'

'That's great. What is it?'

'Pork marinated in porto and cooked with garlic and thyme.'

'Are you sending Larkins some of that?'

'You're joking, aren't you? That's reserved for my close friends and family at the moment. It's a secret. Understood?'

'Promised,' Ian said with his hand over his heart. 'Not a word.'

He closed the container.

'I'm nearly finished here,' Jack told him. 'We can't all finish at four o'clock like you teachers.'

'The kids are doing their homework?'

'I wouldn't count on it. We'll see in a moment. How are they doing at school? Are they paying attention?'

'They're doing fine. They're making good progress. You should be proud of them.'

'That I am, Ian. But the thing is, I can't let them know it, can I?'

He smiled to himself as he garnished the meat tray with parsley and carefully wrapped it until it was airtight. He took his apron off, dropped it into his washing basket, and started sterilising his work utensils.

'Is Emily home?'

'She's upstairs with the lads. Go and see if they're doing their homework if you like. I'll be up in couple of minutes.'

He climbed the steep flight of stairs that separated the butcher shop from the home.

'How are you, Ian?'

'I'm fine, Emily. Yourself?'

'I can't complain. Jack's finishing up is he?'

'He'll be up in a minute. He's just completed Larkins's order. Are the boys home?'

'They're still out playing. They'll be in soon. They'd better be or I'll send teacher out to pull them into line.'

'The poor lads. They must be sick of seeing me all the time.'

'They should count themselves lucky. Some teachers couldn't care less about their pupils.'

'Unfortunately, that's all too true.'

Ian remembered his Year Ten history teacher; a man who showed no sign of wanting to encourage his students to get excited about what should have been one of the most interesting subjects on the curriculum. The problem wasn't a lack of knowledge or understanding on the educator's part. Indeed, as far as Ian could recall, Mr Wilkinson knew every important date in British history from Caesar's landing to the construction of the chunnel and had published a highly regarded thesis on the loss of national identity in the post-colonial era. The problem lay in the fact that he simply didn't enjoy sharing what he knew and loved with a class of teenagers. Ian knew that being a good academic was only part of what it took to be able to teach. The students spent most of their time in class doing activities in their textbooks while the teacher sipped tea and browsed his own personal reading material. Ironically, Mr Wilkinson unwittingly inspired Ian to pursue a career in education by providing the then sixteen-year-old with a negative example. Ian decided to become both an accomplished academic and an invested teacher.

'You're a lucky man, Ian. Tonight, I'm going to treat you to Jack's latest creation,' Emily teased, stirring the contents of her frying pan.

'Is it the pork with porto, garlic, and thyme?'

She shot him a look of surprise.

'I tried some on my way up here just now. Your husband couldn't help letting the cat out of the bag. It's absolutely delicious.'

Emily shook her head and smiled as she looked into her oven.

'He's such a show-off. He couldn't even wait until dinner to unveil his new recipe.'

'I brought a bottle of Bourgeuil,' Ian said.

'Thanks. That will go very nicely with the meal. So tell me, what's new with you?'

'Not very much really. Everything's fine at school.'

He considered asking Emily if she too had heard the rumours about a new librarian coming to town but thought better of it. He didn't want to encourage his friends to constantly discuss his lack of a private life. It was already enough to handle having a meddling neighbour and a mocking colleague, however well-intentioned they were.

'Life in Mirebury,' he added with a sigh. 'You have to love the place for its tranquillity, but you can't help hating it for the same reason.'

'I know what you mean.'

Emily turned the oven back to a hundred and eighty degrees.

'It's always been like that here, ever since I can remember, and I doubt it's ever going to change.'

Ian nodded. 'I suppose you're right.'

4

The evening sun was sinking low, almost touching the treacherous earth that formed the western boundary of Mirebury. Around the outskirts of the town were a number of farming properties, interspersed with small areas of woodland, but beyond was moorland. The sheep within the stone walls that surrounded the fields glowed pink as they stood staring intensely at nothing at all.

The owner of one of these small properties was in town. He had a problem with the gearbox of his Range Rover so had gone to see Gavin Kemble, the town's mechanic. He knew Gavin would give him the most reasonable price possible to do whatever had to be done. Being overcharged was seldom a problem at any of the town's businesses. His wife was also in town. She worked in a boutique where she sold handmade wool clothes, and although she didn't make much of a living out of it, she thoroughly enjoyed having her own shop and chatting with friends who dropped in from time to time. Her two sons would come to the shop once they'd had enough of playing football and the three of them would go home together.

What neither the farmer nor his wife knew was that an intruder was taking advantage of their absence to rummage through their property and make away with several of their belongings. They would be thankful that the burglar hadn't stolen their new flat screen TV, or the boys' Nintendo Switch. And the wife's few but rather valuable items of jewellery would also be exactly where she'd left them the last time she'd touched them. Indeed, it would take the farmer almost a week to discover that a theft had even taken place, because the target of the thief was not the property's stone cottage but the small tool shed hidden behind it. A place where the farmer kept all kinds of bits and bobs, much of which he rarely used.

With a gloved hand, the thief seized one of the tattered wooden shafts leaning against the stone wall and lifted it carefully to see what type of tool it was.

A shovel. No good.

He raised another shaft.

This one was a digging spade. Perfect.

He glanced around the dark shed.

There was a wheelbarrow, its tray ravaged by rust and peppered with holes. He could do with that, despite its poor state, but it would be too difficult to take with him. There were others he could easily get hold of elsewhere, and that would be untraceable.

He spotted a sledgehammer and grabbed it, and then found a digging bar jammed behind an old spare door. He took that too.

These were all the tools he needed to get the job done. It wouldn't be easy by any means, but it would definitely be worth the effort. Years of frustration and procrastination were finally about to be put to an end. He'd thought this time had been wasted. But now he was convinced he'd been subconsciously preparing himself. Now, the time was right and the ideas were ripe. The hypotheses that had nagged at him for so long were ready to be put to the test. As far as he was concerned, an idea denied the chance to be realised was as wretched as a new-born baby denied its mother's teat, and maternal dissatisfaction was a matter he knew intimately, the theme song to the thief's life in his own view.

He wrapped the tools in a dirty blanket and headed towards the door of the shed. It hung ajar, allowing a stretch of sweet pink light to flow into the gloomy interior. He listened, but there was no sound. He then peered outside, looking left, then right.

There was nothing. Just fields of daydreaming sheep.

With the blanket tucked tightly under his arm, he ran along the side of the house, paused again, and then darted off the property. But just as he was about to cross the street, the sound of an approaching vehicle alarmed him. It was coming quickly and he didn't have enough time to find somewhere to hide.

Before he knew it, the car had driven past, leaving him to watch it disappear behind the next bend in the road.

He hadn't been noticed. That was fortunate. But he could easily have been. Greater care would be required from now on. He made a mental note of that.

He looked left and right again, dashed across the road and into the woods, and escaped into the moorland beyond.

5

Jack poured two drams of Talisker and passed one of the glasses to Ian.

'What do you have planned for this weekend?'

'Nothing special. I've got homework to mark.'

'Rocking lifestyle, mate,' Jack grumbled, shaking his head.

'You have plans?'

'I wouldn't mind heading off for the day on Sunday, out of town, I mean. I can hardly remember the last time I got away from Mirebury. It's not healthy, is it? You can almost forget there's a world out there, beyond the moors.'

Ian sipped thoughtfully at his whisky. He often felt the same way, but his friend must have felt it even more keenly. Ian had chosen to leave London. The city had never been the right environment for him. It wasn't so noticeable as a teenager and at university, but once he'd entered the workforce, and especially after his girlfriend of four years had left him, the desire to make a clean break became more urgent. He had accepted the job in Mirebury, willingly trading the city for a small country town. Jack hadn't chosen. Mirebury was all he'd ever known.

'I understand, Jack. Every now and then, you need to go to a place where you're a complete stranger. You need to be incognito and unnoticed and free. You need to breathe.'

Jack raised his glass to that.

'You've hit the nail on the head. I wish I had your way with words.'

'It hasn't served me all that well, Jack. After all, you're the one with a wife and kids.'

'Come off it, mate,' Jack said cheerily, giving him a friendly punch on the arm. 'You'll find a good woman. But you're probably going to have to venture beyond Mirebury to find her.'

'A mission for Sunday?' he suggested, then drained his glass.

Ian laughed. He knew Jack was right. It would do them both some good to get away.

'I'll let you decide where to go. Surprise me.'

Jack grabbed the whisky bottle and served another glass, winking conspiratorially.

'Slow down. Dinner will be ready soon,' Emily told them, somehow knowing her husband had poured another round even though she couldn't see them from where she was. 'The lads should be in by now.'

'I'll see if they're out front,' Ian offered.

He went to the window overlooking the street and saw the boys kicking their football around. He opened the window momentarily, just long enough to tell them to come inside for dinner without letting too much heat escape the house.

6

The midnight hour had come and passed, and the town of Mirebury found itself lost in a shroud. Most of the inhabitants were wrapped up in bed and sleeping soundly. The farmers had been asleep for hours, having hit the hay not long after the fowl in their coops had tightened their talons around their perches. It was the same story for the baker and his son, as well as for Jack. Ian had long since walked back to his lonely home, finding his way back through the fog without difficulty. Even with low visibility and too much alcohol in his blood, the familiar route between Jack's home and his own was as easy to follow as footprints in deep snow. In bed, curled up in his comfortable duvet, he was sleeping the way a man with a clear conscience and a full belly deserves to sleep.

All was dark across the street at Mrs Hopkins's house. There was no doubt she was sound asleep, having recited the Lord's Prayer and said goodnight to the photo of her husband that watched over her from under the lamp on her bedside table.

Only five people in Mirebury were awake at that time of the night.

Vernon White was having difficulty getting to sleep because he was suffering from a rather nasty cold. Every time he dropped off into the land of nod, he almost immediately coughed himself awake again. His wife, who nobody in town would ever describe as being a patient woman, had had enough of the interruptions to her own attempts to get some rest and asked him more than a little firmly to be so kind as to go and continue coughing and spluttering on the sofa in the living room. Vernon had done as she suggested, switching the television on and muting it, then making himself a cup of tea with a dollop of honey and a dash of lemon juice. It was a futile attempt to distract his mind and soothe his sore throat, but he did his best to take comfort in the hot drink and black-and-white western.

On the other side of Mirebury, in stark contrast to Vernon's plight for warmth and relief, somebody was wide awake and out in the cold. The figure was hidden in a hooded raincoat and practically invisible in the thick fog. A dry grating sound disturbed the still air and the hooded head turned as though attempting to see if there was anybody about to hear the noise. A moment later, he slipped past a rusty wrought-iron gate.

The task that was about to be undertaken was one which would be highly risky. It would not, of course, be the first time that somebody had done such a thing, but it was without doubt an action the likes of which was not heard of on a daily basis. The advantage of doing something that others have already done before is the reassurance of knowing that it *can* be done. On the other hand, that doesn't mean that everything will necessarily run smoothly during the performance of subsequent attempts. The man in the dark raincoat coat kept these considerations in mind. The accounts he had studied relating to how the task had been carried out previously gave him confidence.

The first priority would be to work as noiselessly as possible. The only sign indicating his presence that could conceivably reach the nearest houses was that of noise. Light should not be a problem since he only needed a weak torch, and it would only be used close to the ground. Furthermore, the fog would prevent any stray light from penetrating even far enough to reach the stone walls surrounding him.

Time would be of minimal concern as it was extremely unlikely that another living soul would happen to waltz along until well after sunrise, which was more than seven hours away.

He moved forward slowly but without hesitation, knowing where he was going. He had already identified the exact location of his worksite. The lay of the land had been memorised, it was just a matter of walking the right number of yards and turning left at the right place, and always remembering the first priority, not to make too much noise. He made sure not to drop the tools that were wrapped in the blanket tucked tightly under his arm.

The moist gravel squelched rather than crunched under the boots of the nocturnal visitor. As he made his way into the cemetery, the surrounding headstones drifted into view, row after row. There were crosses, granite slabs, here and there an angel, blind and impotent. Many of Mirebury's inhabitants would have been scared out of their wits strolling through such a place during the witching hour. They would imagine ghouls or goblins crouching unseen around them. But he didn't fear mythical beings. Beneath the hood was a scientific mind. The only thought that bothered him was that he might be caught by somebody alive and kicking; by a person strong enough to hold him fast, and quick enough to avoid a blow from one of the heavy tools in his possession. He feared being stopped before he'd accomplished what he intended to do, before he'd become an important figure. He couldn't allow himself to be stopped while he was still worthless and insignificant.

As he approached his target, he switched his torch on, holding a hand over the light until it was close up against the surface of the headstone in front of him.

He knelt down, holding the torch to the slab, and followed its edge, looking intently as he passed the light along the perimeter.

After a few seconds, his hand stopped and he allowed himself a brief smile.

'There you are.'

Jenny Somers was the third person awake. She'd been sleeping soundly, but a noise had woken her. She was certain it hadn't been a dream. It had come from upstairs. She listened for a moment, trying to hear past the heavy breathing of her husband, Mitchell, who was sleeping like a log after a long day working with his sheepdogs. She listened for footsteps, but as the muffled sound of an upstairs window being stealthily closed reached her ears, she knew that it was too late for footsteps.

She got out of bed as quickly as she could without making too much noise or any abrupt movements. She didn't want to wake her husband because he needed his rest and could do without worries during the night. Jenny wasn't concerned that a thief was in her house. The very idea of a thief in Mirebury was preposterous.

A quick dash brought her to the front door. The air outside was chill and bit at her body, but she ignored it. She saw a shadow fade into the fog down the street and started to pursue it, but she soon gave up the chase. Her daughter was too light-footed for her. It was hopeless.

It was a routine Jenny was used to now, and she knew she couldn't beat her opponent. She wanted to scream out at her daughter. She sometimes felt like calling her horrible names, not to hurt her, but to make her think about how she was behaving, but she held her tongue.

Jenny closed the front door and took a deep breath. She let the wave of anger pass over her, and tried to calm herself. As angry as she was at her daughter, she was far angrier at the despicable creature manipulating her. Jenny wasn't a hateful woman, but hate was the only word she could think of to describe how she felt about him. The world would be a better place without people like that.

She went upstairs to her daughter's bedroom, turned the light on, and had a look around, sighing at the lace curtains and empty bed. She wanted to cry, but didn't. Instead, she accepted defeat again, turned the light off, and crept back downstairs.

Alison Somers was better known as Cherry to her friends, due to the unnatural colour of her shoulder-length hair. She was an only child, just seventeen years old, and should have been at home in her pink wall-papered bedroom, protected by an entourage of stuffed toys. She was somewhat of an enigma, even more so than most teenage girls. In terms of both habit and appearance, she was an incongruous mélange of youthful sweetness and teenage rebellion. It wasn't unusual for her to cuddle her teddies, pick flowers, listen to death metal, and smoke a joint all in the same day. She wasn't much into schoolwork but had a hands-on approach to the study of biology, and the happy targets of her interest in the subject had been numerous. She'd experimented with Luke Brown, Aiden Hart, and Wayne Harding before moving on to Mirebury's resident deviant, Art Rekeby. At first, each of them had thought he was the only study partner she'd ever known, but the illusion had been short-lived. She'd tossed them aside like cigarette butts from a car window, leaving them fuming, useless, and unwanted. Their subsequent feelings for her were a mess of desire and disdain, lust and loathing.

Word of her nightly wanderings had reached the ears of many of the townsfolk and was spreading quickly. This growing reputation didn't seem to bother Cherry in the slightest, but it was starting to take a toll on her parents. Her father heard all about it through his wife, Jenny, who heard the other women talking about what they had heard their children discussing.

'Roll over!' Art told her.

In a blur of fiery hair and snow white skin, she turned onto her stomach and smiled back at him cheekily.

'That's it. Oh yeah, don't move an inch.'

Art snapped a few photos of her and then crawled across his bed until he was behind her.

She spread her legs and looked at him mischievously.

Art angled his camera carefully, framing his delicious subject perfectly.

The flash went off, capturing her two broad smiles.

Cherry moved a little and struck a new pose, sliding her slender fingers into view and opening herself ever so slightly to allow just a teasing glimpse of the moist pinkness inside.

Art took another photo and looked at it on the display screen. She was an absolute stunner, and the shot was flawless in every way. He had immortalised Cherry in a precious moment in time. Whatever was happening or had ever happened anywhere in the world seemed so petty and irrelevant. All that mattered was that instant of pure heaven, together in his room, and beyond the walls could be infinite void for all he cared. He enjoyed taking pictures of her almost as much as the act of sex itself. He had shots of her in all sorts of positions, as well as in different places. He sometimes took photos of the two of them together, but they were mostly of Cherry by herself; posing on his bed, dancing to the radio, taking a shower, even on the toilet. When he'd first started taking shots of her, she'd been surprised and found it weird. None of her other partners in her short but eventful sexual history had been interested in that kind of foreplay. But she'd soon became accustomed to his antics and found it more than a little flattering.

Cherry told Art that if she ever found out these photos were on the internet, she would tell her father and that he would probably kill him. The truth was that she wouldn't have minded at all. It was more of a dare than a real threat. The idea that she could enthral thousands of men all over the world was terribly exciting. Married fathers and pubescent schoolboys, rich businessmen and poor students, fat men and thin ones, handsome and ugly, all stroking their erections and spilling their semen, quivering as they thought how perfect she was, and how much more powerful and captivating than the world's greatest works of art.

Art knew it. He wasn't half the fool people took him to be. He pretended to take her seriously, but he didn't believe her for a minute. At any rate, it didn't matter, because he had no intention of sharing her with anybody else. He kept the images for himself and appreciated them when he was alone.

'Art,' she whispered.

'Hmm, yeah,' he answered absently. He was too busy scanning through the dozens of photos he'd just taken to pay much attention to the real Cherry.

'Put the camera down for a minute.'

She bent her knees and stretched her arms out in front of her, lifting her milky body until her buttocks were up in front of him. She was like a pagan priestess worshipping a deity. But as Art looked up, he knew that any deity would have gladly swapped ends with him.

He tossed the camera aside and grabbed Cherry by her slender hips, drawing her up against him.

'You're my favourite kind of dessert,' he said.

'What's that?'

'Cherry tart.'

She looked back at him with a blank expression on her porcelain doll face.

'Shut up with your stupid dirty talk and take me!'

Art didn't need to be told twice. He bit his bottom lip to make sure his mouth wouldn't ruin everything by releasing any more pathetic utterances, gave her a little spank, and entered her.

7

By the time Mrs Hopkins had finished her breakfast and filled in the remaining blanks in the previous day's crossword, the fog had dissipated and the sun broken through. She drained her cup of tea and stood up, deciding it would be best to go for a morning stroll and run a few errands while the weather was fine. There was no knowing how long it would stay like that.

'Where on Earth did I put that list?' she asked herself, and wandered fruitlessly around the kitchen a few times before continuing her search in the living room.

There was a great deal of baking to be done for the Saturday market, and the first step would be to buy the required ingredients.

She turned on the living room light, but that didn't help. The shopping list was nowhere to be seen. Completing crosswords and winning games of Scrabble didn't pose too much of a challenge to Mrs Hopkins's aging mind, but she often forgot what she'd done with simple household items. The potato peeler, lint brush, and TV remote were constantly straying. An idea suddenly came to her and she took her coat from the stand by the front door. She slipped a hand into a pocket, then another, and found it in the third.

'There it is, you silly old bat,' she admonished herself.

That morning would be a busy one. She had some shopping to do, cheques to deposit, a book to return to the library, and lunch with a friend. Mrs Hopkins checked that she had everything she needed before wrapping a scarf around her neck, putting her coat and bonnet on, and leaving the house.

As she crossed her front garden, she reminded herself that she would have to spend another hour or so weeding if she had the time and energy that afternoon. The green heads of weeds were already starting to pop up around the stems of her well-tended flowers and shrubs. No matter how often she dug the weeds out, paying special attention to removing them with their roots intact, they just kept returning from the dead. She eyed them with annoyance as she opened the gate.

She started along the quiet street leading to the centre of town, where the church bell tower rose above a muddle of mossy slate roofs. As she admired the battlements, caressing the blue sky, she thought about what the Good Book had to say about weeds. There was something in Genesis, wasn't there? Something about weeds, she wondered, as she passed the empty houses in her street. Most of her neighbours were of working age. It *was* Genesis, wasn't it? She was forgetting her Bible verses. More and more often, she got the different books mixed up, especially those of the Old Testament, which had never been as important to her as the New Testament. But there was definitely something about weeds, and she was quite sure it was early on in the Good Book, possibly around the time of Adam. That must be it, part of the first man's punishment for having tasted the apple, or pomegranate, or whatever it was from the forbidden tree. It must have been when he was expelled from the Garden of Eden that poor old Adam found himself introduced to the troubles of the real world. Annoyances like flies in his kitchen, weeds in his garden, and maybe a little arthritis in his fingers. If she happened to see Father Godfrey in town, she would ask him to set her straight on the matter. He would know exactly what the Bible said about weeds and in which book to find the relevant passage.

Mrs Hopkins noted the state of the other gardens in her street as she made her way. These people's forefathers must have made a dozen bottles of cider with all the apples they had taken from the forbidden tree, judging by the way they had been punished with weeds.

She mounted the two steps to the bank, taking care because centuries of use had worn smooth ruts into them, and opened the door to find the manager alone behind the counter.

'Good morning, Mary.'

'How are you today, Vernon?'

Vernon White, the manager of Mirebury's only bank, was one of Mrs Hopkins's closest friends. He'd grown up with her late husband, who had crossed the Channel with Vernon's older brother back in the dark days when Adolf was reshaping the map of Europe. Both Mary's future husband and Vernon's brother had made it back home, and they had remained friends until their final days, often reminiscing together about those mates who hadn't been so lucky.

'What can I do for you today?'

'I have a couple of cheques to deposit, Vernon.'

She handed them to him.

'You should drop by some time for a cup of tea. Anne was just saying the other day that it's been a while since she last saw you.'

Anne's idea of a while was less than two weeks. But in a town where most people who wanted to see each at all usually crossed paths every few days, that did indeed amount to some time.

'How is Anne's head?'

'She's been doing better this week. Not too many headaches. It must be my turn now. I think I might be coming down with a cold.'

'Always the way, isn't it? I would go and say hello to her now, only I'm rather busy this morning,' Mrs Hopkins explained. 'I need to do my shopping and start preparing cakes for the market.'

'You'd best head off then, dear. We'll see you on Saturday.'

'Bye, Vernon.'

No more than a few yards along the same street was the library. Mrs Hopkins, an avid reader, made at least one stop there every fortnight. It was a small library and the selection of reading material was rather limited, but whenever she wanted a particular title to read, it was possible to have it sent over from another library in the county.

'Good morning, Mary.'

Terence Harding had been the librarian for more years than

Mrs Hopkins could remember, and it was with great hesitation that he was leaving his job for retirement. He was by no means a young man, just a few years younger than Mrs Hopkins herself, and he'd made the decision to retire now and travel a little on the continent while he and his wife still could.

'Good morning, Terence. Are you counting down the days yet?'

He offered Mrs Hopkins a smile and held something up in front of the old tweed jacket that he seemed to wear every day. It was a small cardboard calendar and there were several columns of red crosses marked on it.

'Does that answer your question?' He laughed.

'Have you met your replacement yet? She's a pretty young thing according to the rumours.'

'No, not yet, but as you say, she's a young lady. She might do a better job at attracting more folks in here than I've been able to do.'

The library was usually empty during the week except for a few kids after school hours. There was seldom a huge rush for books during the weekend either.

'When does she arrive?'

'Next week. I'll have just enough time to show her the ropes before I finish up.'

'Well, I certainly look forward to meeting her, but I shall miss you, Terence.'

'Don't worry about missing me. I'll still be here in Mirebury, and I have a sneaking suspicion that a great deal of my time will be spent here in the library on an unofficial basis.'

'That's good to hear.'

'I'll only be away for a few months, visiting some of the sights Europe has to offer.'

'That ought to be lovely. Where are you planning on going?'

Terence was pleased Mary had asked him that question.

'The itinerary hasn't been written in stone yet, but most of the trip is already planned. We'll take a ferry across to Normandy and drive to Etretat. I've always wanted to visit the "French Dover".

After that, we'll head down to Mont Saint-Michel, before leisurely making our way to Paris, visiting a few Loire châteaux along the way. After a week in the city of lights, we'll go to Burgundy to sample some red wine and travel south to Italy to spend a while in Florence, Venice, and Rome. I was thinking about going to Spain, but we opted for Vienna and Prague instead. We haven't decided how to come back yet, but we'll probably travel through Bavaria, back across France and take a ferry in Brittany.'

'That sounds like quite an adventure!'

'I hope so. I've been wanting do it for years.'

Terence noticed the book that Mary held in her hand. 'Been doing some cooking for the market, have you?'

'I'm going to get started today. I found some good ideas in this little publication.'

She handed him the book and he checked it out for her.

'I'd best get going. I have a lot of shopping to do today.'

'See you on Saturday. You don't need me to remind you that your cakes are the highlight of the market.'

'Don't be silly, Terence.'

'I wouldn't say it if I didn't mean it.'

'You're too kind.'

'Not at all. Take care of yourself now, Mary.'

She headed outside and set course for her next destination, the grocery shop, where most of the town's residents did their shopping. As she walked, she noticed a bank of grey clouds looming over the horizon and decided to get her shopping done and get to Delia Deane's house as quickly as possible. She'd been invited to lunch, but it wouldn't matter if she arrived early. It turned out to be a wise move. The downpour began shortly after she'd reached Delia's house, and it went on like that for nearly three hours. She waited until it had stopped before going home.

By the time she'd opened the gate to her garden, she was thoroughly tired and didn't feel like doing the weeding or preparing her ingredients. The thought of sitting in front of the television and nodding off to an old film was much more appealing.

She closed the gate behind her and put her bags on the ground so she could check the post. She lifted the lid of the red letterbox and looked inside.

There were no letters, but there was an object of some kind. It was difficult to make out what it was. It didn't look much like a parcel. She looked more closely. From above, it looked round and smooth like a ball but seemed to be made of a hard whitish material.

Without really being aware of what she was doing, she found herself reaching into the letterbox with both hands.

Once it had been lifted clear, she realised what she was holding. A gasp escaped her mouth, and a look of utter terror spread across her face. She looked all around, as though expecting to find whoever had made the delivery standing nearby, observing her in silence. But there was nobody. The street was as deserted as usual.

She didn't know whether she ought to go out onto the street and seek help or scurry into her house and securely lock the door behind her. In any case, she felt incapable of doing either.

Her head started to spin and she let go of the gruesome thing between her hands, dropping it back into the letterbox with a loud clang.

What kind of twisted person would put such a thing in a letterbox? And whose was it?

No sooner had those two questions begun rebounding inside her head than she guessed the answer to one of them. Her mind went blank, her weary knees buckled, and she collapsed in a heap on the wet ground.

8

There was really no way for Mrs Hopkins to judge how long she'd been lying on the ground when she came to her senses. Her first realisation was that she'd fainted. The sensation was a strange one, and she couldn't for the life of her remember the last time anything of the kind had happened before. It wasn't the same as going to bed at night and waking up in the morning, not even like waking up in the middle of the night. Coming back to one's senses after fainting was entirely different. There wasn't only the awareness of the passing of an undetermined length of time, but also the feeling of being displaced. It took her a moment to understand where she was.

Her second realisation was that she felt frozen to the core. Rain had soaked her clothes and skin. She didn't seem to be hurt from her fall. In fact, the idea of just staying where she was would have appealed to her if it hadn't been for the cold.

As she struggled to her feet, grasped at her shopping bags, and hobbled towards her house, Mary Hopkins didn't think about what had happened and couldn't actually remember why she had passed out. All she was able to think about was getting herself and her baking ingredients into the dry warmth of the house and taking a hot shower. Her behaviour was instinctive. The questions would pose themselves later.

She forced herself to get up and get inside, concentrating hard on what she was doing, on every step she took. She made sure to lock the door behind her and placed a hand on the walls to steady herself as she made for the bathroom.

Once warm water was flowing from the shower head, she stepped into the enclosure and stood there for a while with her eyes closed and the water sheathing her like a chrysalis. It got the blood flowing in her veins and the thoughts flowing more readily through her mind.

She wondered if anyone had seen her in such an unsightly and undignified state. It was impossible, she told herself. Absolutely impossible. If any of her neighbours had seen her like that, they would have come to her aid. Her neighbours were all good folk.

Those words stayed in her mind as the water streamed down her weary face. *All good folk.*

The image of what she'd found in her letterbox flashed onto the insides of her eyelids, vague like a dream of being at the cinema, but with a violence that made her shoot her arms forward in search of the white tiled walls of the shower enclosure. She thought she was going to faint again. Perhaps her neighbours were decent and kind people, but if it wasn't a neighbour who had left that terrible surprise for her, who was it? She really couldn't imagine how *anyone* would be capable of doing something like that.

She had to call Sergeant Manning. This was a police matter. She knew that. But first, she had something else more urgent to do.

Ian arrived home from school just as Mrs Hopkins was leaving her house. He was reaching into his pocket to fetch his key when he heard her front door being closed. Even from where he stood on the other side of the street, he could see there was a problem.

'Mrs Hopkins,' he called out. 'Is everything all right?'

She stopped in her tracks like a surprised mouse. After an awkward moment, she simply shook her head at him.

'What is it?' he asked, this time quietly, so quietly she couldn't hear his voice at all.

She pointed at her letterbox without uttering a single word.

A chill ran down Ian's spine. It reminded him of how one of his pupils, Miranda Forbes, had pointed at the door to the girls' toilets one day. After being asked what was wrong three times, she'd told him that even though she desperately needed to use the facilities, she didn't dare because there was a monster inside. Ian had gone to find Liz and she'd verified that there were no monsters in the girls' toilets whatsoever, just a headless Barbie doll prostrate beside the hand basin and several hair bands and ribbons on the floor. But the same posture and attitude seen in his elderly neighbour was far more disturbing, especially since Mrs Hopkins had always proved to be a very sensible lady.

Ian crossed the street, keeping his eyes on Mrs Hopkins. But hers remained fixed on the old red letterbox. She was petrified.

'Why on Earth are you staring at your letterbox, Mrs Hopkins? Is there a monster in it?' He laughed uncomfortably, but stopped when he saw she wasn't amused in the slightest.

She turned to him and seemed to look straight through him, as though the real world had become transparent, and for an instant, Ian had the impression he'd ceased to exist for her. Then she spoke, giving him a normally simple instruction to follow.

'Take a look for yourself, young man.'

Ian approached, confused and on edge. It was just a normal letterbox. Mrs Hopkins opened it every day that mail was delivered. It was ridiculous to be afraid to look inside it.

He told himself to get a grip as he reached for the hinged lid. Every day after work, he opened his own letterbox. The old dear must have found a spider inside hers. That was bound to happen from time to time. But she wasn't the kind of woman to be frightened of a spider, was she? Not the kind found in Britain.

With one swift movement, he opened the letterbox and looked inside.

Of all the potentially disturbing objects he could have imagined, he would never have guessed what he could now clearly see.

'It's a *skull*.'

He stood back, without taking his eyes off the letterbox. Then he turned to Mrs Hopkins, as though expecting her to provide some logical explanation.

'There's a skull in your letterbox,' he repeated.

She allowed herself a fleeting smile.

'I'm not insane then,' she said, a glazed look on her face.

'No, you're not. But somebody bloody well is! Who would

play such a macabre joke?'

'A joke? I hardly think it's a joke.'

'What does it mean? Have you called Sergeant Manning yet?'

'Not yet. I want to go to the cemetery first.'

'You think it's a skull from the Mirebury cemetery?'

'Obviously!' she snapped.

Ian was speechless. He'd never heard Mrs Hopkins speak so sharply before. Then again, it was the first time she'd ever found human remains in her letterbox.

He dug into his coat pocket and pulled out his smartphone.

'We'll make our way to the cemetery and I'll get Sergeant Manning to meet us there,' he suggested as calmly as possible.

She gave a single solemn nod and looked him straight in the eye, showing him she'd managed to pull herself together.

He peered into the letterbox again, just to make sure he wasn't mistaken. But, of course, he couldn't be. They couldn't have both hallucinated.

It was still there, an inanimate object blissfully unaware of the psychological affect it caused. He gently closed the lid. But somebody was aware, unless it was children's mischief. Not likely though, was it? Where would children get their hands on a human skull?

They walked together, Ian holding her by the arm to support her. He held his smartphone in his free hand. Once Sergeant Manning had been convinced Ian wasn't playing some kind of joke on him, he promised to be at the cemetery immediately after passing by the house to inspect Mrs Hopkins's letterbox. Judging by the sound of his voice, Ian suspected the policeman was slightly happy. There was seldom anything of interest for a sergeant to do in a town like Mirebury. Now he had an extremely unusual affair to handle. Ian could forgive his excitement, but he'd best not let Mrs Hopkins notice it.

He hung up and slipped the phone away, a frown forming on his brow.

'Mrs Hopkins, I'd like you to answer a question if you're willing to do so.'

'Yes. What it is, dear?'

'Do you think you know whose skull it is?'

She turned away from him, and it seemed to Ian that she started to cry. In his six years living in Mirebury, he'd never seen her shed a tear.

'If I answer your question, will you stop saying that horrid word?'

'If you like.'

'I'm convinced it's his, Ian. It's my husband's.'

He stopped walking, obliging the widow who was holding firmly onto him to do likewise.

She drew a deep breath and made herself stop crying.

'How do you know that?'

'I don't know how I know.' She started walking again. 'I just do. I can feel it.'

They continued in silence, both asking themselves endless questions but articulating none of them.

Mr Hopkins's resting place seemed to be intact. The headstone stood where it had been since it was erected the day his widow tucked him into his eternal bed. The slab that covered his grave was exactly where it should have been, and the flowers that Mrs Hopkins had recently offered her sweetheart still bore their petals and were still in the solid vase that stood upon the concrete slab.

'Everything appears to be in order, doesn't it, Mrs Hopkins?'

She studied her husband's grave. If anybody knew every detail of that burial site, she did. She leaned closer and Ian supported her.

'Yes.'

Ian looked around. Nothing stirred. The place was dead still. Of course it was. Only the mocking crows that peeped at the mourners from the trees surrounding the cemetery caught his attention. Mrs Hopkins continued staring at the grave, mesmerised by it.

'Do you come here every day?'

She shook her head. 'Not every day. Not quite.'

'How about we go back to your house and I make you a cup of tea?'

'I thought it was him, Ian. Thank goodness it's not.'

'You had a nasty shock, Mrs Hopkins. If ever I lay my hands on the creep who did that...'

'Come now, Ian,' she said, a faint smile appearing. 'You're not the violent type.'

He felt a rush of annoyance and winced. He was a gentleman, and proud of it. He was calm and unassuming, and content to be so. But he was a man of principle, and he was no coward.

'Maybe I'm not. I'm not wired that way. But I think that in certain situations I would be capable of sorting someone out.'

She smiled again, and however condescending it was, he was glad to see her frown disappear for a second.

'Mary!' The voice belonged to John Phelps, the cemetery caretaker. He was as old as the hills but as strong as a mountain. Many of the townsfolk joked that he'd spent so long among the departed that he'd built some kind of immunity to death. He was already older than many of his residents had been when they moved in.

'How are you, John?'

'I'm fine, Mary. But what about you? I can't begin to imagine. Sergeant Manning told me the news. It's horrible! You must think I'm incompetent to allow such an abominable act to take place under my guard. I'm so very sorry, Mary. I don't know what I can say to make you forgive me.'

'Hold on a moment, John. I'm the one who owes an apology. I was mistaken. You see, Clive's grave hasn't been touched after all. And even if it had, I wouldn't blame you. This is a cemetery, not Buckingham Palace. I don't expect you to stand guard around the clock.'

He sighed, relief making his haggard face sag even more.

Mrs Hopkins looked as if she was going to start crying again.

'Now, now, Mary. Don't cry. It was all an innocent mistake. It's good news Clive's resting place hasn't been disturbed.'

'Yes, it is. It is, John.'

Gravel crunched and they turned to find Sergeant Manning weaving his way through the alleys.

'Mrs Hopkins, I promise you this maniac is going to be punished severely!'

'That's good to hear,' the caretaker answered. 'But apparently it isn't Mr Hopkins after all.'

'Really?' the sergeant said. 'Why do you say that?'

'His tomb hasn't been touched.'

'Let me see.'

He knelt in front of the slab and examined it carefully.

'There's no need, sergeant,' Ian assured him. 'Mrs Hopkins is certain nothing has been disturbed.'

Sergeant Manning continued his inspection regardless, and it wasn't long before he discovered marks on one side of the concrete.

'John, are these scratches normal?'

The caretaker knelt beside him.

'No,' he whispered, a frown creasing his brow. 'That's not normal. These are recent marks. You can see how clean they are.'

Both men looked up at Mrs Hopkins.

'Ian,' the sergeant said sternly. 'I want you to take Mrs Hopkins home.'

She protested.

'That's an official order,' the young man informed her. 'Please, just go home. Ian will look after you and I'll come to see you as soon as possible.'

She knew she had no choice. Her head was spinning. Her moment of relief had vanished. Maybe it had been her husband's skull after all. She felt like fainting again.

'Come on, Mrs Hopkins. Let's go and have that cup of tea.'

'What exactly are we going to do?' the sergeant asked once Mrs Hopkins and Ian were out of earshot. 'I mean, we can't just exhume the old boy like that, can we? There must be a specific procedure for this kind of situation, but I've never had to do anything of the sort before. I don't know how to go about it all.'

John looked at the sergeant with an air of impatience.

'It depends,' he said.

'Depends on what?'

'It depends on whether you want to wait weeks for a decision to be made by someone who doesn't know or give a rat's arse about poor old Mrs Hopkins or you want to be able to tell her the truth about what she found in her letterbox by the end of the day.'

John stopped speaking and scratched his leathery chin. He shot the sergeant another look of impatience.

'You tell me what you think is best, Sergeant Manning, and I'll do it. After all, you're the protector of the just and honest in this town. I just bury the folks when they croak.'

Sergeant Manning hesitated. It would be risky from a professional point of view to act hastily and in conflict with the law. On the other hand, the longer it took to discover what had happened, the greater the chance that the madman behind this atrocious act would escape.

'Mr Phelps,' he said, looking the old man in the eye. 'This is between you and me. We won't talk to anybody else about the details of the exhumation. Do you understand?'

'Of course I bloody understand. I'm not as daft as folks think. Now help me fetch the bars and let's get to work!'

It wasn't easy prising the concrete slab off the grave, even with two men performing the task. If someone had opened the grave recently, he would have had a hard time doing so, unless he hadn't been alone. Dirt fell from the crack between the slab and the walls below it.

The scraping sound of concrete against concrete was horrible. The men pushed down on their bars over and over again until, sweating and sore, they succeeded in lifting the lid. They had managed to lift it just a fraction of an inch, but it was enough.

'Pull!' John growled.

They twisted their arms in unison and the slab turned. It was now just a matter of pulling it far enough aside to allow an inspection of the grave.

Mrs Hopkins's hands shook as she tried to sip her tea.

'I don't know why I bothered waking up this morning. What have I done to deserve this punishment? All my life, Ian, I've sought to be a good woman, to treat others with respect. Why would anybody want to wish me ill?'

'I don't know, Mrs Hopkins. I would like to be able to tell you what's happening, but the truth is, I have no idea. One thing is for certain though; there isn't anyone who could have a grudge against you. It must have been a random act.'

'Maybe, Ian. I'm not certain. If it's my Clive...'

She couldn't bring herself to finish the sentence.

'I know. In that case, it must be personal. We have to admit that. Somebody who knows who you are, where you live, and where your husband is buried.'

'If it is him, I don't know what I'll do. It would almost be like losing him all over again. I simply couldn't bear having to bury him a second time.'

Ian wanted to say something reassuring. He searched for the words that would make Mrs Hopkins feel better. But he couldn't find them. The fact of the matter was that they simply had to wait for news from Sergeant Manning. It was a matter of time. What would happen afterwards remained a mystery. If it wasn't Mr Hopkins's skull, they would have to find out who it belonged to, and if it was his, they would have to formulate a list of suspects. It would be a very short list indeed. In either case, it was clear that Mirebury was going to be the target of an intrusive police investigation.

'Can you see the coffin?'

'Yes.'

'And it's closed?'

'Yes.'

'So that means his remains haven't been disturbed.'

'Not necessarily. There's a problem.'

'What?'

'I can see the coffin.'

46

'I don't follow.'

'I can see the coffin. That's the problem.'

'How is that a problem?'

'By rights, there ought to be six foot o' dirt between me and it.'

'Of course,' the sergeant said, feeling foolish.

'That's a bad sign, that is. Strange though. There's no dirt anywhere around the gravesite. Makes you wonder what the blighter did with it all. There should be a big mound.'

Sergeant Manning studied the length of the alley but couldn't see any dirt, just the gravel and grass that paved the way throughout the cemetery. He walked around a little but found no trace.

'So what do you know; we've got a tidy grave robber on our hands.'

'Very bloody tidy. There must have been quite a worksite here. I don't know how I didn't spot it. I'm getting old and useless, I am. Soon it'll be time for me to jump in one of these holes m'self!'

'Don't be so hard on yourself. Nobody can be everywhere at once. Are you going to open the coffin?'

'I s'pose I am, unless you want to do the honours.'

Sergeant Manning shook his head.

'I didn't think so. Where's me ladder?'

The sergeant passed it to him.

'Hold on firmly while I clamber down there.'

He held on and watched John descend into the dark hole. He opened the rotten coffin unceremoniously.

The young policeman felt queasy. That must be normal, he figured. A normal human reaction to an unnatural situation. Old Phelps, on the other hand, didn't seem to be overly bothered by what he was doing. The sergeant wondered if this wasn't his first time digging someone up, but didn't dare ask.

'What do you see?'

'Nothin' much,' he called, switching on his torch. 'That's better. It's empty! Real empty like. There's not a bone to be found.'

John brushed the flanks of the hole with his torch, making sure he hadn't overlooked any clues. But there was nothing except for dirt and decaying wood.

'I'm coming up now. Hold her steady.'

'How am I going to break the news to Mrs Hopkins? She was right after all. The instant she saw that skull in her letterbox, she knew whose it was.'

John grunted in agreement as he reached the surface. He couldn't help but feel partly responsible. It was his role to keep Mirebury's cemetery protected and he'd failed. He shook his head to himself and pulled a tattered pack of Marlboros from his shirt pocket.

'You find this bastard, young sergeant. You track him down. I want to see *his* skull. I tell you what, and you won't mind me saying off-the-record and all. I tell you I'd be more than happy to dig him a mighty deep hole.'

9

The Saturday market was an important event in Mirebury. But it was off to a rather bad start. The news of Mary Hopkins's ghastly discovery had already spread through the town like the Plague. Never before had a scandal of the kind ravaged Mirebury, and from the moment the market opened, everyone knew they were all thinking the same terrible thing. They were wondering whether the maniac was there, hidden like a wolf in sheep's clothing. Despite the unexpectedly good weather that weekend, a dark cloud hung over Mirebury.

After hearing the news, Jane Hopkins, Mary's daughter, had requested time off work and rushed to see her mother. She'd packed her bags quickly with a couple of changes of clothes and toiletries, and driven to Mirebury from her home in Wiltshire. She'd decided to stay with her distraught mother until the affair had been well and truly sorted out, however long it took. Her husband, who adored his mother-in-law and couldn't help but feel guilty for having taken her only child away from her, understood and supported her decision.

This took a load off Ian's mind, because he'd been afraid he would be obliged to keep Mrs Hopkins company himself, and although he cared greatly about her, he couldn't bear the idea of being stuck with her night after night, helping her with crosswords and baking in a futile attempt to keep her distracted. He felt a little ashamed of his reaction, but he reminded himself that Mrs Hopkins would be far better off with her daughter by her side.

Sergeant Manning had taken the skull and was keeping it under lock and key at the modest Mirebury police station until the appropriate experts could come to examine it. He was at the market, eager to prove that he was present and primed. He was speaking to Ian, John Phelps, and Jack Fuller about what they thought would happen to the skull. It now seemed obvious to them that it belonged to Clive Hopkins, but there would still need to be an official identification.

'It looks like we're going to have to postpone that little excursion we were planning, Jack,' Ian said glumly.

'I'm afraid so. It just wouldn't be right of us to go running off now. Mary's going to need all the support she can get.'

'We'd all do well to stay put,' John put in. 'No knowing what's in store.'

'It's unlikely any fingerprints will be found on the skull, don't you think?' Ian asked the sergeant.

'Highly unlikely. Untreated bone isn't smooth enough for prints,' he stated confidently.

'Did John tell you we found all the dirt excavated from the site?' he continued.

They shook their heads.

'Spread out among the trees outside the cemetery, it was,' John said. 'There were barrow tracks in the dirt. Won't help much, mind you. They were the same as mine and just about every barrow in town. We all bought the same model for a steal through Aiden Hart, who has a contact in the hardware business.'

'For the record, I didn't hear that last bit,' Sergeant Manning stated, guessing the nature of the arrangement.

'Could one man have carried out such a mammoth task overnight?' Jack asked.

'Do we know it happened in one night?' Ian cut in.

They looked out each other blankly.

'We don't know shit, I'd venture to say,' John observed. 'Let's assume, for argument's sake, it did happen in a single shift. Well, maybe it's possible for one man. I could have got the job done twenty years ago.'

'Who is it?' Jack asked. His hard gaze swept the market. 'Who are you?'

That was the question, and considering the lack of suspects and apparent clues, it was anyone's guess. They shared a sense of powerlessness, but they were determined to see justice done.

'We need to make an oath,' Jack said. 'We need to promise each other, just the four of us, right here and now, that we won't stop until we've done everything humanly possible to catch this monster.'

They placed their hands over their hearts and promised.

Bang!

Everyone jumped. There was an instant of fearful silence. But it was just a stray balloon that had popped.

General laughter broke out when everybody realised they were being ridiculously nervous, but the laughter remained uneasy.

'The town has been upset by this more than people are willing to let on,' Ian said once he caught his breath again. 'It's as though we're all expecting some madman to walk into the park and start shooting us down with a shotgun, or clubbing us to death with poor old Mr Hopkins's femurs.'

'It's ludicrous,' Jack added.

'Maybe it is. I mean, I hope it is. But a few days ago, I would have found the idea of finding a skull in a letterbox silly too. I don't know what to expect now.'

'Poor Mary,' John said.

'She certainly is putting on a brave face,' Ian observed. 'She's gone ahead with her cake stall all the same. Having her daughter here is helping her morale immensely.'

Sergeant Manning cast an eye about. People were looking at him, no doubt wondering how he was going to deal with the situation. He felt the pressure building. He wasn't prepared for a crime like this, but he couldn't let the townsfolk know that. He met their gazes and nodded reassuringly. They had to think he was up to the challenge.

'Who would have committed such a despicable crime?'

Sergeant Manning knew all the locals, and they knew him. He was on friendly terms with most of them, and a handful of them, including men like Mitchell Somers and Brett Greyson, were very close friends who he knew he could rely on in the most difficult of situations. Naturally, he had a handful of minor enemies too.

From time to time, he had to haul one of the lads into the lockup for the night over a drunken fistfight, but he couldn't imagine any of them digging up a widow's husband. That was just plain twisted. These were plain-speaking country boys, not inclined to deviousness.

'It can't be one of us,' Ian answered. 'It has to be an outsider. That's the only possibility. Nobody in Mirebury would have done *that*. Have any of you noticed an unfamiliar person around town recently?'

'Nobody.'

'No.'

'Me neither.'

'Let's go and get a beer at the farmers' pavilion,' Ian suggested. 'If we're going to think this through, we'll need to lubricate our minds.'

Mary and Jane Hopkins were overwhelmed by the support they were receiving. Mary was selling her baked delights left, right, and centre. She was aware that the added attention and sales were probably out of pity as much as out of a genuine appreciation of her scones, fruit cakes, blueberry muffins, and shortbread biscuits, but it made her happy all the same. The stunned and distracted look that had taken hold of her since the discovery was beginning to wear off.

'Mary, my dear old girl, what's wrong with the world?'

It was Anne White and she was on the brink of crying.

'It's simply horrible! What pathetic excuse for a human being would do such an atrocious thing! It's unimaginable! A man works and fights for king, country, and family all his honest life, and this is what he gets in return!'

'I know, Anne. I don't understand any of it. I'm so eternally grateful for all the support I've received. That's the silver lining, I suppose.'

'Oh, you're wonderful, Mary. Stiff upper lip and carry on regardless. We all admire you so.'

'She's right, mum. Honestly.'

'Jane?'

'Yes, it's me. How are you, Mrs White?'

'I haven't seen you in such a long time. You've grown up into a beautiful young lady.'

'Thank you. But it hasn't been all that long, has it? A year or two at most.'

'Oh, I don't know. I lose track of time so easily. How's your husband doing?'

'Just fine.'

'Any little ones on the way? If it's not too personal to ask.'

'We're working on it.'

The women laughed, and Anne inspected Mary's goods.

'Give me one of those fruit cakes, Jane. Oh, and I'll take four muffins.'

'With pleasure. That'll be three pounds, please.'

'Here you are. See you later then, and look after your dear mother, won't you?'

'She does, Anne,' Mrs Hopkins cut in. 'She's been a great help.'

'Good to hear. Come by my place when you have a chance, the two of you.'

A steady flow of customers approached the baked goods stall, lured by the aromas floating through the crowd. Mrs Hopkins had counted on breaking even, a return on investment as Vernon would say. But with every passing minute, it seemed like she would finish the morning with her goods sold out and quite a nice profit in the piggy bank.

'Hello, Mary. Keeping yourself out of trouble, I see.'

It was Doctor Sykes, the town's tall and powerfully built general practitioner. He would have been dashingly handsome if it hadn't been for the incessant bashing his face had endured during his rugby days. Nevertheless, he was a fine example of manhood, and he continued to look after his physique. He was with his equally attractive wife and his two daughters, who were eyeing Mrs Hopkins's shortbread biscuits with hungry green eyes.

'How are you feeling?'

'I'm fine, Gordon. Physically, at least.'

'The physical and the mental are linked, Mary. You know that. If you want to talk, you should come and see me at the surgery. In fact, even if you don't think you want to talk, you ought to come all the same. Monday morning's looking quiet.'

'Thank you, doctor.'

'There's no *thank you* about it. You come and talk to me first thing Monday.'

'I'll make sure she does,' Jane promised him.

'Good. In the meantime, how about a dozen scones?'

'And shortbread biscuits,' the girls sang in unison.

'A dozen of those as well.'

'I'd better go now,' Jack declared during a pause in the conversation. 'The old girl is holding the fort over at the meat stand. I should really be there with her. If the customers ask difficult questions, she won't know what to say and I'll be in trouble for having abandoned her.'

He made a point of finishing his ale and putting the glass down heavily.

'All right, Jack. I'll come and see you later. I need to pick up my order anyway,' the sergeant told him.

'I'd better leave you as well,' John Phelps said after finishing his pint of ale. 'I can't help feeling I should get back to the cemetery. There are just too many living bodies around this place for my liking. No, but seriously, I keep asking myself, what if this happens again? I mean, this may not be an isolated incident. I have this nagging notion that while I'm here with the rest of Mirebury, this maniac is out there in the empty streets of our town, or in my cemetery, roaming free and wreaking havoc.'

The others froze. They hadn't thought of that. Almost all of Mirebury was at the market. The streets, shops, and homes of the town were entirely unprotected. The perpetrator of the crime, if he was not one of those at the market, might be out there taking advantage of the quiet to do whatever hideous deed he had in mind.

'You're right, John,' the sergeant agreed. 'I should get into my Rover and drive around for a while, check out Mrs Hopkins's place. Sorry, Ian, looks like you're going to be left all alone with the shepherds.'

'Not likely. I'll go along with Jack to see how his meat is selling. Let me know if you come across anything and need a hand.'

'Same here,' Jack said.

'Can you drop me off at the cemetery, young man?' John asked. He stuck a badly needed cigarette in his mouth and felt his pockets for a lighter.

'No problem. And thanks, Ian. I'll let you know if anything crops up.'

Ian caught up with Jack as he reached his stand.

'You bloody well took your time. How long does it take to drink a pint?' Emily asked loudly, aiming to embarrass him, and succeeding.

Ian cut in before they could start arguing.

'How are you, Emily?'

'I'm all right, Ian, but I'd be doing better with a bit of help.'

The meat stand was beautifully arranged. Pork, lamb, and chicken sausages were lined up neatly, steaks and lamb chops were laid out in concentric circles. Ian even spied a few morsels of the scrumptious delicacy he'd eaten at Jack's house a few days earlier. It seemed the butcher had changed his mind about reserving it for friends only.

'You've done a fine job of managing the meat stand, as always,' Jack told her, nodding appreciatively.

His compliment was met with a cold glare.

'Get your chubby arse over here and help me.'

'Yes, dear.'

He rolled his eyes at Ian, making sure Emily didn't notice.

10

The next week began slowly, and with an air of palpable distrust. In the streets, outside the school, at the shops and pub, people looked sideways at each other. They asked themselves if they really knew their neighbours. They carried out their various duties but sought to only speak to their closest friends and family wherever possible, avoiding those against whom they held a grudge or harboured even the slightest suspicion.

Jane took her mother to see Doctor Sykes on Monday morning, just as she'd promised. It did Mary some good. Gordon was comforting and advised her to force herself to continue her daily routine, with the exception of visiting her late husband's desecrated gravesite until the affair had been resolved. He informed her about the medicinal options available but strongly suggested not resorting to them unless she felt it was absolutely necessary. She assured him it wouldn't come to that.

On Tuesday, an investigative team arrived and spent most of the day behind closed doors with Sergeant Manning, Mary Hopkins, and John Phelps. Afterwards, these three were questioned by the locals, but they kept their lips sealed, as they had been instructed to do. In any case, there wasn't much to say.

The cemetery was thoroughly scrutinised, but to no avail, and within a week, the identity of the skull would be verified.

But everybody already knew whose it was.

Mitchell Somers went to the school on Wednesday morning to talk to Ian's class about his sheepdog training techniques. The visit had been planned weeks in advance and there was no reason to cancel it. Quite the contrary. Ian wanted to keep their minds off what had happened.

'Boys and girls,' he announced after morning tea, 'I would like you to warmly welcome our special guest, Mr Somers. He is, as

I'm sure you know, Mirebury's reigning sheepdog champion.'

Ian clapped as Mitchell Somers entered the classroom with his dog, but the children hesitated.

'Come on! You can do better than that. I said *warmly* welcome Mr Somers.'

At seeing his beautiful dog, Drover, the youngsters became more enthusiastic. They jumped up from their seats and ran towards the working animal. But one girl, who was sitting near the front of the classroom, found herself far too close for her liking and started screaming hysterically.

'Stop!' Ian said loudly.

The group swarming around the dog completely ignored their teacher's order.

'You'll scare him,' Ian told them.

'It's not a problem, Ian. Drover has a good temperament. He's really very friendly with children.'

'Calm down, Suzy. Drover's a disciplined sheepdog,' Ian said. 'He's a champion.'

He tolerated the excitement for a moment before telling the students to return to their seats. They did so, slowly and not without complaining.

'Let's be quiet now. Shhh!'

'Good morning, boys and girls,' Mr Somers greeted them.

He wore a broad smile, the same he'd worn since learning the prize was his again.

'Good morning, Mr Somers,' the pupils replied.

'Mr Somers,' Ian explained, 'won the sheepdog trials last year. I know that most of you were there at the show. I saw a few of you shooting tin ducks and running in the three-legged race. What I want to know is whether any of you happened to see Mr Somers or the other competitors with their magnificent dogs. Do you remember?'

A few hands shot up.

'What did you think?'

'It looked difficult,' one of the boys suggested.

'That it is,' Mitchell Somers agreed. 'It requires a lot of work and patience.'

'What's your dog's name?'

'Drover.'

'Rover? Like the four-wheel drive?'

'No, Drover, with a *d*?'

'What does that mean?'

'That's a good question. A drover is a person who leads livestock over long distances from one property to another. It's a word commonly used in Australia, where *long distances* can mean many hundreds of miles.'

The mention of that vast land on the other side of the world raised their eyebrows. Ian knew some of them hadn't yet travelled even as far afield as London.

He was going to ask Mitchell to tell the kids all about sheepdogs in an attempt to get them talking, but it seemed they had plenty of questions already. Hands were waving vigorously in the air. Mitchell, who was generally a man of few words, had prepared a little speech for the occasion, but it looked like it wouldn't be needed after all.

'What's the most important factor?' Owen asked. 'I mean, in order to be a good dog handler.'

Ian gave the boy congratulatory nod.

'Well, first you need to train the dog. That's the first step. Then it's all a matter of the relationship you have. A sheepdog isn't a pet, but a colleague.'

Mitchell looked around the class, waiting for other questions.

'Is your daughter called Cherry?'

Mitchell was taken aback by the unrelated question, and didn't know how to react. He hurried to fill the awkward silence.

'Yes,' he admitted. 'Her real name is Alison.'

Whispers and murmurs spread throughout the class, making Ian and Mitchell look at each other, confused.

'Do you know her?' Mitchell asked the boy who had brought up the new subject of discussion.

'No, but my big brother does,' he replied, feigning innocence briefly before grinning at his mates.

'So what?' said one of the girls, not quite aware of the real import of her words. 'Your brother's not the only one who knows her. Lots of the older boys do.'

The room exploded into laughter, yelling, and rude comments.

'My big brother knows her good and proper.'

'I love to pop cherries!'

Ian and Mitchell were speechless.

'I've heard she has more sausages in her every day than Fuller's shop in a year!'

Mitchell Somers blanched.

'She sucks better than a Dyson!'

'That's enough!' Ian yelled.

The children sometimes played up, but he'd never seen them treat a visitor so rudely before. He too had heard rumours of Cherry Somers's insatiable sexual appetite but was unaware that the younger children of the town knew about it.

'Be quiet!' Ian ordered in his most serious teacher voice. 'I'm utterly disgusted at this appalling behaviour.'

The laughing subsided.

'I think I'll be leaving now,' Mr Somers announced sheepishly.

He wasn't angry, although maybe he would be later. He just seemed stunned and embarrassed. His voice was that of a father who felt hurt, and who didn't doubt that the horrible words and accusations were true. If only he could train an adolescent girl as easily as he was able to train his fine dogs. But he was powerless, and he and everybody in town knew it.

'Mitchell,' Ian began, not knowing what to say. 'I'm sorry.'

Ian turned to the class. 'I want everybody, and I mean *everybody*, to apologise to Mr Somers *now*!'

Some students apologised, while others protested that they hadn't even opened their mouths. Meanwhile, Mitchell Somers fled the classroom with Drover at his heels.

'I have never heard such disgusting talk in all my life. It's an outrage! You are all going to wish you hadn't done that! We're going to have a long meeting with the headmaster and your parents!'

11

Ian had trouble sleeping that night. At difficult times such as these, he sometimes thought about whether the support of a loving woman would provide a comfort. He always came to the conclusion that it would, that he would be able to sleep more easily with a companion in his arms. It had been so long since he'd been in a real relationship that he could no longer quite remember what it was like. He'd forgotten how it felt to share his bed. It left a gaping void in his life, an incompleteness that made his daily routine seem meaningless. There were men who were suited to bachelordom, but he wasn't one of them. During the day, he could ignore it, but at night the emptiness nagged at him.

Lying alone in bed, he tried to avoid dwelling on his situation, and instead found himself thinking alternately about Mary Hopkins and Mitchell Somers.

Mr Somers had told Ian he didn't blame him for what had happened in class, and he appreciated that. He always felt responsible for what happened in his classroom. He believed that a disorderly class was invariably the result of an incapable teacher. He didn't tell his pupils that. They were young and immature and would take advantage of his self-criticism. Ian had made it clear to his pupils that he blamed them entirely for their misbehaviour, and he had already taken measures to reprimand both the class as a whole and the worst offenders in particular.

He nodded off for a few minutes at a time but then woke up to find his memories of the previous few days gnawing like rats at the back of his mind. This happened repeatedly throughout the night. He fell asleep then found himself waking up again shortly later. He kept looking at his bedside clock to check what time it was. Part of the problem was that he didn't know whether to think about the terrible day he'd had at school or the more disturbing issue of Mr Hopkins's skull. He didn't really want to think about anything at all, but his brain had its own ideas.

Turning his back on the glowing clock beside him, he closed his eyes once again and managed to fall asleep for a while.

The next time he woke up, he knew it wasn't because there were rats nibbling at the walls of his mind's busy corridors. There was a more direct cause. For a moment, he could have believed there were real rodents somewhere in his house, but he quickly realised this was not the case. The high-pitched, rhythmic sound that had disturbed him was coming from outside. It was faint, but it was growing louder by the second. If he'd been able to sleep deeply, the sound would have come and gone unnoticed.

He lifted his head off the pillow, ever so slightly, so he could hear more clearly. The noise was growing louder, as though whatever was causing it was drawing nearer. It disturbed him more than he cared to admit. He couldn't shake off the feeling that it was coming for him, whatever it was. It continued to grow steadily until it seemed it would eventually find its way into the house.

Then it stopped.

The otherwise normal silence felt heavy now. Its sudden return had been unexpected, and the cause of its disruption remained a mystery.

It was two forty-three.

He crawled out of bed and went to his bedroom window. His curtains were thick and the night was very dark, so he could hardly see where he was walking. He almost slipped on a magazine he'd left lying on the floor. He cautiously drew the curtains open, just enough to see outside.

The street was deserted, as though the sound and whatever had made it had simply vanished. He scanned his front garden, the street, and the houses across the street. Despite the darkness, he could tell nothing was out of place in front of his house. Likewise, Mrs Hopkins's house was still and dark. The two women inside were probably fast asleep, or maybe tossing and turning in bed just as he had been.

Only shadows occupied the street, and there were no lights on in any of the houses that could be seen from his bedroom window.

He began to wonder if it had all been a hallucination; the effect of loneliness, an overactive imagination, and the anger and confusion caused by the abhorrent thought that the people of Mirebury could no longer completely trust each other.

'What's that?' Ian gasped, and opened his eyes wider.

One of the shadows had just moved, or so it had seemed. He focused his attention on it.

It moved again, barely noticeably.

A shiver tingled on the back of his neck before crawling spider-like down his spine. Within an instant, his pulse had accelerated and he found himself breathing more quickly.

His view of Mrs Hopkins's house was incomplete. He could see the slate roof, whitewashed walls, and lightless windows, as well as her front door. But he couldn't see the gate to her garden, and he couldn't see her letterbox. He couldn't see them because a dark form was obscuring his view.

It moved again, turning towards him.

He pulled his face back from the window instinctively, afraid that the shadow would notice him watching.

The faint grating noise started up again, and as he peered between the curtains, he saw the shape move away. It didn't move very quickly, but it moved smoothly, as though floating away, until it disappeared from his field of vision. The faint noise faded with the dark figure that accompanied it.

It was a bicycle. As simple as that.

He was afraid. He wanted to stay inside his bedroom, safe and sound. But he couldn't. Somebody, or some kind of shadow, had just stopped outside Mrs Hopkins's letterbox.

What was in there now? More of her husband's remains?

He couldn't afford to pretend it wasn't a big deal. He knew he had to ignore his fear and get out there. He had to confront this madman. He would never forgive himself if he just crawled back into bed like a coward. Mrs Hopkins had told him he wasn't a violent person. She'd laughed at him when he'd suggested he was capable of sorting somebody out. He had to prove her wrong.

There was a bat under his bed. He seldom played cricket, but he remembered it was there. He reached under and fumbled around until his hand fell upon it. He grabbed it, stumbled through the dark, out of his house and into the cold night. He was half-naked but now fully awake, and the crisp air made him shiver even more.

The street was deserted and all trace of the bicycle and its noisy chain was gone. He looked in the direction the shadowy figure had taken, but it was too late. The scene had returned to its usual state of emptiness and heavy silence.

'Who are you?' Ian whispered to himself.

He looked across at Mrs Hopkins's house. He had no idea who could hate her enough to want to terrify her like that.

He'd missed his opportunity. It was too late now, too late for tonight at any rate, but maybe he'd come back another night. He almost longed for him to return. He would be ready next time.

He swung his cricket bat around in his fidgety right hand. One good swing would have been enough to overpower the creep. Just a single decent blow to the head.

He walked across the street, heading straight for Mrs Hopkins's letterbox. The normally harmless household recipient of letters, bills, postcards, and junk mail crouched threateningly in the dark. He didn't know whether to open the letterbox or smash it to smithereens with his bat. Its dark slot looked like a devil's grin mocking him, daring him to be foolish enough to come closer.

It's a fucking letterbox!

He stepped up, drew a breath, and opened the metal lid.

There was something inside.

A chill crept through him. It was too dark to identify the object inside, but there was definitely something, and he was pretty sure it wasn't a scented letter from one of Mrs Hopkins's pen friends. Reaching into the void of the letterbox was absolutely out of the question. What if it was a trap? What if he ended up with his hand mutilated by a spring-loaded steel spike or a nice little sulphuric acid bath? His imagination ran riot. It wasn't worth the risk. It would be wiser to get a torch so he could see what had been placed inside without having to touch it.

It only took him a minute to rush back into the house, find a torch, and return to the letterbox. He made sure he carried out the task as quietly as possible because he didn't want Mary or Jane to hear him. They didn't need to know about this delivery. The old dear had already suffered too much.

He held the torch over the letterbox, but even before he'd switched it on, he knew there was a problem.

He gasped, unable to believe what had happened. Then he looked up and down the street. His heart was beating faster again and he began frantically shining his torch into every dark corner around him.

The letterbox was empty. Whatever had been in there was now gone. He would have questioned his sanity if he hadn't been so sure an object had been there just a minute earlier.

His grip tightened on the cricket bat. His knees began to shake nervously, and his eyes darted everywhere. It seemed impossible, but in the brief moment it had taken him to find a torch, the contents of the letterbox had been removed. That surely meant the shadowy form he'd seen was still nearby, watching him from a hidden vantage point, laughing at him silently, taking delight in the fearful confusion displayed by the half-naked man wielding a bat.

'Where are you?' Ian hissed into the night.

Silence.

The bat was now swinging in his right hand, and the torch in his left hand was following the erratic movement of his eyes. He wanted to shout out a challenge. He wanted to tell the hidden figure to show himself and fight it out like an honourable man, even if that meant that one of them would not survive the night. But he didn't want to disturb his already distraught neighbour. Above all, not that.

Instead, Ian reluctantly decided to go back to his bedroom and keep watch from his window in case the Postman returned.

In a way, he'd won that particular battle. Even though he hadn't managed to apprehend the Postman, he had, at least, foiled his plan to make a delivery.

Slowly and guardedly, he walked back to his house, making sure to close the door properly behind him, and positioned himself behind his bedroom curtain. He stared at Mrs Hopkins's letterbox until he couldn't stay awake any longer, then he crawled into bed and slept as best he could until dawn.

12

Sergeant Manning had been instructed to question everyone in town about the crime. As the day progressed, his police four-wheel drive could be seen parked outside different houses and businesses. He was trying to gather as much information as possible about what had happened, but thus far had established nothing beyond the fact that the skull did indeed belong to Mr Hopkins. What he really wanted to hear was that at least one of Mirebury's residents had observed some kind of strange behaviour leading up to or following the discovery. He needed a lead to follow. His plan of attack, as in any investigation, had been to start by speaking to those most likely to have relevant information. He had, of course, already spoken to Mrs Hopkins and her daughter at length, but they were as shocked and baffled as anybody else. He'd already spoken to Ian at the market, and they had spoken again by phone that morning when Ian called to share what had happened during the night. As far as they were aware, this was the only sighting of the Postman.

Vernon White knew why the sergeant was there when he entered the empty bank just before lunchtime.

'Hello, Sergeant Manning. Do you have any news?'

'No, Mr White. I was hoping maybe you could help me with that.'

Vernon's face was as blank as a new chequebook.

'I'm afraid not. I haven't noticed any strange folk about town.'

'You know Mrs Hopkins better than anyone. I'd be right in saying that, wouldn't I?'

'I suppose so. We've been friends for years, and I greatly respected Clive. He was one of the finest men ever to come out of Mirebury.'

'You can't think who would want to hurt her like this?'

'No, I can't. Absolutely not. Nobody in town could answer that question. You know as well as I do that we're all fond of her.'

'Except maybe one person,' the sergeant suggested.

'You think it's one of us? A Mirebury resident?' Vernon asked, raising his eyebrows, defying the policeman to confess to such a ludicrous belief.

'I don't think anything for the moment, Mr White. I hope it's somebody from out of town, but hope has nothing to do with it.'

'I've been thinking about it as well. I've tried to imagine who could want to make Mary suffer. It's simply unfathomable. This isn't the work of sane mind. There's no rhyme or reason to this crime. Can't be. It must be the work of complete nutter,' he went on, shaking his head in futility as he spoke. 'I can't think of a motive. Money? She hasn't got much. Revenge? She's never hurt a soul in her life. Revenge against Clive? He might have offended a Nazi or two back in the day, but he was loved by one and all this side of the Channel. Random lunacy, I tell you. It has to be an out-of-towner. Let's hope he's moved on already. I don't know. You've got a hell of a mystery on your hands.'

The sergeant gazed around the bank for a moment, then turned back to Vernon and looked him in the eye.

'Mr White, has Mrs Hopkins ever borrowed money from the bank? Does she have, for example, a debt she can't repay?'

Vernon was speechless. Had the young sergeant really just asked him what he thought he had?

'What the bloody hell do you mean? What a ridiculous question! No. As far as I know, Mrs Hopkins doesn't owe anybody anything, and even if she did have a debt with the bank, I wouldn't dig her husband's bones up to convince her to settle it, would I?'

'I know, Mr White. I'm not throwing mud or suggesting you have anything to hide, and I certainly don't mean to cause you distress. All the same, these questions have to be asked. It's standard procedure.'

67

Vernon doubted Sergeant Manning knew much at all about standard procedure. He took a deep breath, and calmed himself.

'Very well. Now I've answered it for you. I know you have your questions to ask, but like you said, I'm one of Mary's oldest friends.'

'I know. You don't have any information you think might help?'

'Nothing. Nothing at all. Just promise me you'll do your utmost to catch this monster, won't you?'

'I have to be honest, Mr White. It's not looking good. I don't have any leads.'

'If I hear anything, I'll let you know immediately.'

'Thank you. Sorry to have upset you, Mr White.'

'I suppose it can't be helped. We're all on edge. You've got your job to do, and I can certainly appreciate that.'

The sergeant beat a hasty retreat and moved on to the post office to talk to George. Before setting foot inside, he reminded himself to be a little more tactful this time.

The conversation didn't last long.

'I have no idea who would do such a thing. It's pure madness. I'm quite sure her letterbox was empty the last time she had mail. There's always a faint kind of *tink* when I drop an envelope into her letterbox. You know what I mean? I really do think I would have noticed if I hadn't heard that sound. It would have struck me as being peculiar. When you've been doing the same round for as many years as I have, these little details become blatantly obvious.'

'I know exactly what you mean. It's quite the same for me.'

George nodded encouragingly.

'You find this maniac, sergeant. We're counting on you.'

'I'll do my best,' he said, disgusted by how useless he sounded, and took his leave.

By the time the sun had set, Sergeant Manning had spoken to the majority of the town's residents. He spent an average of five or ten minutes with each person, just the time to ask a couple of questions and confirm that the man or woman had no information to offer. Only Ian had seen the Postman, and Sergeant Manning realised that if there was indeed some kind of personal vendetta against Mrs Hopkins, her young neighbour was in an ideal position to help apprehend the perpetrator.

He drove his four-wheel drive back to the police station. He had to write up his daily report before heading back to Mitchell Somers's house—off duty this time—for a beer. It had been a busy but fruitless day. He needed to rethink his approach. He needed to draw up a new plan of attack.

The sergeant wasn't the only one in need of a pint. Headmaster Deane was also keen to wet his whistle. He caught up with Ian as he left the school grounds after a long day of drumming sums and sonnets into the town's young minds.

'Do you have time for a beer, Ian?'

Jonathan Deane was an old-fashioned headmaster and always retained a formal relationship with his staff during school hours. But once the final bell of the day had rung, he was quick to loosen his tie a little.

'Sure, Jonathan. Do you want to talk about Mitchell Somers's class visit?'

His bushy eyebrows arched and his thin lips shrivelled as though he'd just bitten into a sour grape.

'Good grief! I most certainly do not. I want to talk about anything *but* that. I think we've done all we can with regards to that little spectacle. I just want to have a pint of ale. That's all. No ulterior motives, young man.'

'With pleasure. Let's go to The Owl and Moon.'

It was a short walk to the pub, which was just off the village green. Ivy grew across the front of the old stone building, reaching up past the lantern and sign hanging over the green door. Cartwheels leaned against the wall on either side of the entrance, and a solitary smoker sat on one of the wooden benches, staring at his phone. It was Aiden Hart, the older brother of one of Ian's brightest students. He was Mirebury's electrician and general handyman.

'Hello there, Aiden. How's business?' Jonathan said.

The young man looked up but turned his head to blow a cloud of pungent smoke away from his former teacher.

'Hi, sir…I mean, Jonathan.' He laughed. 'Old habits die hard. Work's slow, but I'm paying the bills. I've just been talking to Harry. He needs some work done on his beer pumps and his cold room. That should keep me busy for a while. You two need a pint after putting up with the kids all day?'

'Indeed,' Ian replied.

'I hope they're better behaved than I was,' Aiden said, a glint of cheekiness in his blue eyes. He gave Jonathan a knowing wink.

'You just needed to be a little more attentive, my boy.'

'Yeah, I know. Never too late to learn a thing or two though, is it? I do a lot of reading nowadays, believe it or not.'

'It's never too late,' Jonathan hastened to agree, offering an encouraging smile.

'Owen's doing well, isn't he?' Aiden asked Ian.

'He's a bright lad, and he looks up to you. I'm under the impression he likes staying with you in the cottage and giving you a hand in the workshop whenever he can. You help him with his homework, don't you?'

Aiden released a cloud of smoke before replying, and Ian watched it rise into the air in front of the pub's sign, forming a misty veil through which the silvery owl with outspread wings and the full moon appeared to shimmy.

'I guide him a little but make sure he works all the answers out for himself. I'm really proud of him. Mum's not a good influence on him, and he knows it. That's why he often sleeps at my place over the weekend. She's had a few too many raw deals, been knocked down and not really bothered to get up again. I know what it's like to have your heart broken, even if she refuses to believe that. My job's to teach Owen how to look after himself, and to make sure he doesn't make the same mistakes we made.'

He took a drag of his cigarette and squared his shoulders.

'You're doing just fine, young man. Keep at it,' Jonathan told him firmly.

'Have a good evening,' Ian said.

'Thanks. Likewise.'

They entered the pub, stooping slightly as they passed through the low doorway.

'How are you, Harry? Two Spriggans if you don't mind.'

The pub was still fairly quiet. There wasn't anybody else at the bar. Three men were playing darts, one of whom Ian recognised as Vernon White's nephew, and a couple he didn't know were chatting together by the window. They looked like a married couple on a day trip, or perhaps lovers trysting. It generally wasn't until after five that the bulk of the troops came marching in.

'Ian, I heard about your little adventure last night.'

'You did?'

'I'm a publican, mate. I've got a reputation to keep. But I'd like to get the goods straight from the horse's mouth. What exactly happened?'

Ian told Harry about the previous night's events. He wondered who had told him, realising he probably shouldn't have let the word out in the first place. But it was already too late. If Harry Newcombe knew about it, everybody in town would soon hear the news. Ian promised himself not to say a word to anybody next time. But he hoped there wouldn't be a next time.

'Do you think he'll come back?'

'I suppose he might, but I can't always keep guard.'

Harry wiped the bar dry as he listened.

'I guess you can't,' he agreed. 'It's too much to handle on your own.'

'If it happens again, we'll have to take some kind of orchestrated action,' Jonathan suggested. 'A few men will need to take turns watching over Mary, an hour or two each night. Sergeant Manning can't be expected to be everywhere at the same time.'

'That's not a bad idea,' Ian said, looking from Harry to Jonathan, and then shooting a quick glance at the other patrons in the pub. 'The problem is how to know who we can trust.'

71

'You think this Postman fellow is one of us.'

'I don't know. He could be, couldn't he? We're in no position to rule out the possibility.'

'You're the newest arrival in town, Ian. Maybe it's you behind all this.'

If Ian hadn't known the barman better, he might have been upset by the accusation. But Harry didn't mean it personally. He was just disgusted by the idea that one of his customers or friends could be responsible for such depraved actions.

'Maybe I am, Harry. If you really think that, feel free to stand guard outside my place all night. That would kill two birds with one stone. You could keep an eye on me and look after Mrs Hopkins at the same time.'

'Don't worry, Ian,' he said, smiling. 'I'm having you on, mate. You're just about the last person I'd suspect.'

'At any rate, I doubt I'll be able to sleep much tonight,' Ian admitted. 'I had a hard enough time last night, even before what happened.'

'You know what you really need, Ian? You need the phone numbers of two people who live in your street; one at either end,' Jonathan suggested. 'That way, you can alert one or the other, depending on which direction the Postman takes, and the escape route can be blocked.'

Harry stopped wiping the bar, and Ian's glass froze midway between the table and his mouth.

'Impressive, Jonathan. You're thinking like a real tactician there. John Phelps lives near the cemetery. He could block the nearest exit from Mirebury. But who lives in my street at the end near the town centre?'

'Gavin Kemble does,' Harry suggested.

Ian shook his head. He didn't want to say why he didn't consider that man a suitable candidate for the task in case one of the other clients in the pub overheard.

'No. Who else?'

'There isn't anyone else.'

'Last night, he headed out of town. It makes sense after all. If he does come back, he'll probably do the same thing again. I'll give old Phelps a call later. I'm sure he'll agree to help out.'

'It's in your hands then, Ian.'

'I have to go now,' he announced. 'I've got a book due back at the library today. See you both later.'

'See you later.'

'Ian,' Jonathan called out as he reached the door.

'Yes?'

'Do be careful. I don't want to have to break any bad news to your class in the morning.'

Ian paused, looked Jonathan dead in the eye, and smiled appreciatively before leaving.

13

Ian was unaware the new librarian had already arrived in town, so when he stepped inside and found a pair of well-rounded buttocks displayed right in front of him, he was more than a little surprised. Charlotte was wearing a white blouse and a flattering black skirt over sheer stockings. She was in the middle of stacking gardening books along the bottom shelf of the horticulture bookcase.

Ian was still appreciating the view when she turned unexpectedly.

'Hello,' was all he could manage.

'Hi. Can I help you?' she asked innocently enough, pretending she hadn't caught him red-handed.

'Are you the new librarian?' he asked lamely.

She smiled with equal parts of politeness and mockery at his stupid question and obvious embarrassment. 'Yes, I am. You can come in if you like. You don't have to stand at the entrance.'

'I just arrived.'

'Did you?' she asked, taking pleasure in his discomfort. 'My name's Charlotte.'

'Nice to meet you. I'm Ian. Welcome to Mirebury.'

Charlotte was even more charming face-to-face than she was from behind, bent over a stack of volumes on how to make marigolds flourish judging by what he could see of the covers. Her intelligent green eyes studied him from behind a pair of burgundy reading glasses, and he was sure her smile was discreetly flirtatious.

'The library's closing in a few minutes. If you want to take a book, you'll have to be quick about it,' she informed him sternly.

'I just came to return this one.'

'I hope it's not overdue, Ian. You'll have to pay a fee if it is.'

He laughed. 'I never return books late. You can check my record if you like.'

'Don't worry. I will,' she said, reaching a hand out to him, palm open. It took Ian a second to realise she wanted him to hand her the book.

'*The Master of the Moor.* I don't mind a bit of Ruth Rendell myself,' she said. 'I haven't got around to reading this one yet.'

'You should. It's not bad at all.'

'Are you the local master of the moors?'

'Hardly,' he admitted. 'That would probably be Damian Granger. He lives alone in a caravan out on the moors. I venture out for a hike now and then, but I'm by no means a master. I'm not even the master of my own destiny.'

'That's up to you to change, isn't it? When you see something you want, you have to have the courage to step up and grab it firmly with both hands.'

Ian smiled. He liked the playful tone in her voice.

'That strikes me as being sound advice. I think I'll take it on board and put it to the test the next time an interesting opportunity presents itself. So, how long have you been in Mirebury?'

'I arrived a couple of days ago. Mr Harding has been filling me in on the library system and the town in general.'

'Has he told you much about what's been happening?'

'Not really. Why? What do you mean by that?'

He didn't want to scare her with talk of skulls in letterboxes just yet. That could wait for another day. He regretted bringing it up and sought a way to change the topic.

'Mirebury's a nice town, generally speaking, but it has its quirks. I'm from London myself. I came here about six years ago, and I suppose I'm still getting used to it.'

'Why did you leave London?' She paused. 'Sorry. I'm being a bit nosey. I do that sometimes.'

'It's all right. Me too. I came here for the same reason as you, I guess. There was a position available at the primary school here, so I packed my bags and headed into the moors, curious and eager for a change.'

'No looking back?'

'No looking back,' he confirmed. 'Have you met many of the locals yet?'

'Not really. I've been pretty busy with Mr Harding. As soon as he feels I'm ready to look after the library on my own, he's going to start travelling. He's keen to set off, so we haven't been wasting any time.'

'I can show you around town if you like, when you're not too busy.'

She'd told him to grab firmly with both hands.

Charlotte ran her fingers through her long brown hair and looked away. She looked around the library for a moment and seemed to be contemplating his offer. When her gaze fell upon Ian again, he knew she was going to accept. He could just sense it.

She had a smile that could melt ice.

'Give me a minute to close up.'

14

Jack Fuller was a sound sleeper who tended to snore loudly. With his wife wrapped up beside him and the children asleep in their room, he usually slept until his persistent alarm clock had rung out at least four times. With this in mind, he found it strange that he had woken up in the middle of the night for no apparent reason. He didn't need to go to the toilet, he hadn't been having a nightmare, and his wife was sleeping peacefully beside him. There was no obvious reason behind the disruption.

He closed his eyes again and tried to keep his mind blank. But as he waited for sleep to reclaim him, something caught his attention again. A noise had reached his ears, and it had come from beyond the walls of his bedroom.

He drew a deep breath and held it for a while so he could hear better. But there was no longer anything to be heard. He wondered whether he'd merely imagined it.

He closed his eyes and let his strong body relax.

It was just as he was starting to drift back into the realm of dreams that he heard a sound louder and more singular than before. He knew what it was immediately. There was no mistaking it—the high-pitched chime of the bell that informed him a customer was entering his shop downstairs.

His heart started to pound. He hauled his heavy body out of bed and stumbled through the darkness as quickly as he could. There was no doubt about it. Somebody had broken into his shop with the intention of making off with his fine cuts and homemade sausages.

He stampeded down the stairs as quickly as he could, despite not be able to see where he was putting his feet. The idea that he might be plunging himself into a dangerous situation barely even occurred to him. As far as he was concerned, he was going to catch the thief red-handed and beat him senseless until he was as tender as one of his famous sirloin steaks. After that, he'd call Sergeant Manning and explain how he'd been forced to defend himself against the violent intruder. No doubts would be raised.

His feet served him well. He didn't fall going down the stairs but arrived safely in the shop, where he found himself completely alone.

Soft streetlight penetrated the blinds, and the hygienically clean metal display shelves where he put his goods every morning gleamed against the darkness. All was quiet. Looking around, he found his shop to be exactly as he would expect it to be, except for one eerie detail. The front door, to which the bell he'd heard just moments earlier was attached, was wide open. His shop, and therefore his home, had been violated.

He clenched his fists and stormed outside, ready to unleash hell and hoping it wasn't too late to catch the would-be thief, but nothing disturbed the cold dark night.

He was alone in the street.

For an instant, he wondered if he'd simply forgotten to close the door that evening before going upstairs. Maybe he'd left it open and the bell had been agitated by the wind. Only there wasn't even the hint of a breeze.

No. Somebody had definitely entered his shop.

'You're bloody lucky whoever you are!' he spat into the silent night. 'You nearly got yourself the hiding of your life.'

He calmed himself down, slowed his breathing, and listened intently. For an instant, he thought he heard a grating sound, like that of an old bicycle, but he couldn't be sure. However outraged he felt, he wasn't going to run around the streets of Mirebury in his pyjamas in the hope of catching the thwarted thief.

He went back into his shop and switched the light on.

Whatever the intruder was after, Jack must have scared him away in time. Nothing seemed to be missing. The shop looked as though nobody had been there at all. The door hadn't been damaged, so he figured that either the lock had been picked or he'd forgotten to close shop properly after all. He kept the key hanging from a hook on the wall in the workshop and was relieved to see it was indeed there. He returned to the front door with the key and inserted it into the lock. It turned smoothly and the mechanism clicked into place.

The bugger must have picked the lock, he figured. He decided he'd have to install a bolt in the morning. That would slow him down in future.

'A thief in Mirebury,' he mused. 'It really is beyond belief. What's happening to this town?'

He swung the solid door to his cold room open and was glad to see that none of the meat seemed to have been stolen. There were a couple of sides of pork, one of lamb, and a quarter of beef, all where he'd left them hanging the previous evening. The steaks that had already been cut were still neatly wrapped and stored on the shelves.

He closed the door, shivering under his pyjamas.

There was no need to check his safe because he kept that upstairs in the bedroom, disguised as a chest of drawers. The thief's efforts had all been in vain.

There was no point disturbing Sergeant Manning's sleep. He would mention the incident when he next came to the shop.

He turned the light off and made his way quietly upstairs, deciding it would be futile to try to go back to sleep. Instead, he put his earphones on and listened to music on the sofa, keeping the volume low.

15

The front door swung open and Ian was greeted with a warm smile.

'Thanks for coming, Ian.'

'Not at all, doctor. Thank you for the invitation.'

'It's a pleasure. With all that's happening in town, it's important to get together for a good old dinner now and then. You know, I think the townsfolk don't spend enough time really talking to each other. That might be partly responsible for all this horrible business with Mrs Hopkins and Jack,' the doctor speculated.

He gestured for Ian to enter his charming home and closed the door behind him, trapping the warmth inside.

'Go and make yourself comfortable by the fireplace, Ian. I'll be with you in a moment.'

'Wait a minute. What do you mean about Jack, doctor?'

'Firstly, and I've told you before, you can stop calling me *doctor* all the time. I'm not a time traveller in a phone booth. My name is Gordon. How would you like me to go around calling you *teacher* all the time, Ian?'

'I wouldn't like that one little bit.' He laughed.

'Now, with regards to your good friend, Jack,' Gordon continued. 'I assume you've heard about his adventure last night?'

The doctor raised his eyebrows inquisitively.

'No, I didn't see him today.'

'That's why you need to get yourself a wife, young man. The female of the species knows how to kill two birds with the one stone, or in my case, how to do the shopping and catch wind of the local gossip with one stone.'

Gordon shot a cheeky grin over his shoulder, but Mrs Sykes wasn't in the living room with them to appreciate his sexist humour.

'Talking about women, I'll be asking you all about that fine young librarian you had dinner with last night in a few minutes, so you'd better start preparing your answers now.'

'Thanks for the warning.'

'As for Jack, he had an attempted burglary last night.'

'Someone broke into Jack's shop?'

'Yes.' Gordon confirmed. 'Wait a minute, Ian. Go and sit down. I'll get you a whisky, unless you'd prefer something else.'

'A whisky will do fine, thanks. Here, a little something for you, Gordon.'

'Thanks, Ian. Saint Nicolas de Bourgueil,' he said approvingly. 'That's a nice drop.'

Ian sat down by the fireplace and let the warmth of the flames put some life back into his body while the doctor served their drinks.

Gordon had suggested that the cruel treatment Mrs Hopkins had received and the break-in at the butcher shop may have been part of a broader and obviously subtler change to the moral values of Mirebury's population. Ian felt that he may have been getting a bit carried away with himself, but the idea that the same person may be behind both acts did seem plausible. After all, there weren't many crimes committed in Mirebury, so it was no great leap of the imagination to suspect that a direct link between the two occurrences existed.

'So, as I was telling you,' Doctor Sykes continued, pouring two glasses. 'Somebody broke into Jack's shop during the night. He didn't manage to get away with anything though, because Jack scared him away.'

'Well, at least he didn't take anything. Was Jack all right?'

'He's angry, of course, but otherwise fine.'

'*I* wouldn't like to be caught by an angry Jack in the middle of the night!'

'Me neither,' the doctor said with a chuckle, raising his glass. 'Cheers, Ian.'

Their glasses chimed together.

'Cheers.'

'Frankly speaking, I can't help feeling that we're going to see more of this kind of incident.'

'I know. I'm afraid of that too. I wonder if the same person is behind both crimes.'

The doctor sipped at his whisky.

'Perhaps. Unfortunately, Jack didn't get a look at the intruder. But he said he heard what sounded like a bicycle being pedalled away in the distance.'

'He said that? He heard a bicycle? Just like I heard outside Mrs Hopkins's house the other night.'

'You did?'

'Yes. It would appear Mrs Sykes doesn't provide you with *all* the local gossip.'

'So, it *is* the same person then.'

'Apparently,' Ian concurred. 'In a way, that's good news.'

'How's that?'

'Well, it's better to have just one troublemaker in town than a general breakdown.'

'That's true. Whoever he is, we need to catch this joker before he strikes again.'

'I've already started working on a plan to launch a round-the-clock watch.'

'You have? Let me know if I can help. I'd like to be involved.'

'I'm sure I can find a post for you, Gordon.'

The doorbell rang, disturbing the two men from their discussion. The sudden sound made Ian jump. He was feeling more on edge than he'd realised.

'We'll talk about this later, Ian. It's a great idea. We all need to take an active role in protecting the town.'

The doctor stood up and went to open the door.

Jonathan Deane had arrived, accompanied by Vernon and Anne White.

'Come inside, friends. Thanks for the flowers, Anne. They're lovely.'

As he led them to the living area, he called out to his wife.

'Helen, where are you? Everybody's here.'

Helen Sykes appeared briefly, dressed in her apron and wearing oven mitts. 'Good evening, I'll be with you all in a moment.'

As the evening progressed, Ian was pleased to find that his host had either forgotten to or decided against asking a volley of indiscreet questions regarding his first date with Mirebury's new acquired librarian. At the dinner table, the conversation was centred on the emotional state of poor Mrs Hopkins. The guests wanted the doctor's professional opinion.

'She'll be all right, won't she, Gordon?' Jonathan Deane asked. 'I don't know what we can do help her. There's nothing to say that can console her after what happened.'

'She's in good physical health,' Gordon reassured them, 'but this incident has deeply affected her. As I'm sure you all know already, Mary feels as though she is mourning her husband for a second time, and the worst part is that nobody can tell her *why* this has happened.'

'She's trying to think of somebody they may have offended or hurt over the years,' Ian added.

'That's ridiculous. Mary wouldn't hurt a fly,' Vernon said.

'What concerns me is that her state of mind might cause her health to deteriorate. I insisted that she come tonight but it was impossible to convince her to do so. She just wants to stay at home with Jane. We all need to do our best to cheer her up and reassure her this won't happen again.'

They all nodded in agreement, with the exception of Ian.

'The problem is, we don't know that it won't happen again,' he pointed out.

'I know,' Gordon admitted. 'We can't know for sure until we catch this monster.'

Nobody said a word for a long moment. Every mind was once again ticking over, trying to imagine who could be behind it all. Could it be one of them, one of the people sitting there at that very dinner table?

The quiet was too uncomfortable for Helen's liking.

'There's still plenty of cauliflower with stilton. Don't let it go to waste. Who'd like some more?'

They all politely declined.

'It was a lovely meal,' Ian said. 'I'm not used to eating so well.'

'Thanks, Ian,' Helen said. 'You need to find yourself a nice young woman who knows how to cook.'

He smiled awkwardly, both because her comment was so outdated and because it was the opening of a floodgate.

'Does your Charlotte cook?'

He tried not to wince.

'I don't know. At any rate, it's a little too soon to call her *my* Charlotte. We had a very nice dinner out last night and got along nicely, but for the moment, that's all there is to it.'

'Leave the poor boy alone,' Gordon interjected.

'Yes, of course. We need to let young love take its course. I'm just happy to have some good news to talk about in the village.'

'We can't disagree with that,' Vernon White said. 'This business with Mrs Hopkins has got us all talking nervously and looking over our shoulders. Sergeant Manning has been doing the rounds as well. He even questioned *me* the other day.'

'He's questioned all of us. It's nothing personal. He's just following procedure. He came to see us as well,' Gordon said.

'It's the same thing for all the school staff,' Jonathan added. 'It doesn't mean he suspects one of us.'

'Oh, dear! What's that?' Anne White interrupted. There was a look of alarm in her eyes.

Everybody froze and stared at her questioningly.

'What are you talking about, honey?' Vernon asked her softly.

'I think there's somebody outside. Are you expecting other guests?'

'No, we're not,' Helen answered, almost whispering.

Gordon got to his feet quickly, but before he could move, the front door swung wide open and footsteps sounded.

Helen sighed as her son appeared. 'It's just Tim.'

'What's going on?' the adolescent asked. 'You all look scared stiff.'

They laughed uncomfortably.

'We've got to put a stop to this before we all end up neurotic,' Ian said.

'Are there any leftovers?'

'Yes, darling. I won't let you starve to death,' his mother teased.

'I brought the mail in for you.'

'I got the mail earlier,' his mother said, looking perplexed. 'Was there more?'

'There's just a letter.'

'Who's it from?'

'That's the strange thing. There's no name, address, or stamp on the envelope. It must have been delivered by hand.'

He gave the letter to his father, who opened it with the aid of his steak knife after wiping it clean. He unfolded it, and even before he'd started to read, he realised it heralded trouble. The letters used to make up the handful of words it contained had been cut out of a newspaper.

'Is this some kind of sick joke?'

'What's wrong?' Helen asked.

The doctor's face had turned pale.

'What is it, dad?'

Helen and Tim watched the doctor intently. Ian, Jonathan, and the Whites looked at each other with puzzled faces.

'Helen, didn't you say nothing was taken from Jack's?'

'That's right. Not a single item as far as he could tell.'

'He didn't say anything about his meat being tampered with?'

Everybody gasped, and wondered if they were all going to die right there at the Sykes's dining table.

The doctor put one hand to his mouth, as though trying not to regurgitate his wife's delicious meal.

'Gordon, for crying out loud, tell us what it says,' Jonathan pleaded.

With the other hand, he turned the letter so all present could read it.

The effect of the message was horrifying and instantaneous.

Anne White fainted and fell heavily from her chair, her husband not quick enough to catch hold of her. Ian and Jonathan's faces went pale as they suddenly understood that Jack's intruder hadn't been a thief after all.

DON'T EAT JACK FULLER'S MEAT! HE SELLS HUMAN FLESH!

16

Ian pushed the door to Jack's shop open and the little bell rang.

The place was deserted.

'Jack? Are you there?'

Silence.

'Jack?'

'Come upstairs,' the butcher instructed him flatly.

He followed his friend's voice.

'You've called it a day early?'

'What day? I've hardly sold a thing since I opened. I tell you what, I'll snap his bloody neck the day I catch him. I'm not joking either, Ian. There'll be no calling Sergeant Manning. I'll deal with him myself, and it won't be pretty.'

Ian knew Jack well, and he knew his words were not spoken lightly. As much as Jack could be a best friend, Ian pitied the man who made an enemy of him.

'I had two customers today. Can you believe it? Just two. Old Patterson and Aiden. Maybe they hadn't heard the news. Patterson's hearing's not the best, bless him. At any rate, he wouldn't be bothered about eating human flesh. That old rogue wouldn't care what filled his belly. As for Aiden, he's always tinkering with contraptions in his workshop and most likely still daydreaming about Cherry Somers, like half the lads in town who've had her. He doesn't have a clue what's going on around him.'

'I don't know how everyone found out about the letter, Jack. We decided not to talk about it. We all promised to keep it a secret. Refusing to make the letter public would have taken the sick pleasure out of this psychopath's game.'

Jack nodded impatiently. He clearly had more to say.

'It wasn't just Gordon who received a letter. As far as I know, more than ten of them were posted. According to the sergeant, the wording was exactly the same in each. Letters from the same edition of an unidentified newspaper had been cut out and pasted on sheets of writing paper. There were no fingerprints or hairs to be found.'

'Ten letters? I didn't know. And nobody saw the Postman riding around town.'

'It seems not.'

Ian shook his head.

'A campaign of psychological terror is being conducted against Mirebury. The Postman wants the whole town at his knees, and he's going to get there. We've got to start a watch. He couldn't have done this if we'd had men stationed around town last night.'

Jack sighed loudly as he went to the fridge to grab a couple of beers.

'Why is this happening, Ian?'

'I don't know. It doesn't seem to be personal; not against Mrs Hopkins, and not against you either.'

'That may be. But even if it isn't supposed to be personal, it's my income and reputation that are suffering.'

'No, Jack. Perhaps your income is temporarily suffering, but not your reputation. We all know you're the victim here.'

He sipped at his beer.

'I'm not so sure of that. The worst part is that his sick joke is working. People didn't come to buy meat from me today because they really believe these letters. Half the population of Mirebury is trying to figure out who the flesh could belong to and whether anybody has gone missing recently!'

'You think it's impossible?'

Jack gave him a not-you-too look.

'It's part of the game, Ian. He's messing with our minds. You're smarter than that. Anyway, I may not know much about human flesh, but I know what I sold to Helen Sykes yesterday, just like I know what the left-overs she brought back to show me today were. Top quality beef, that's what. It was Black Angus, Ian. The best beef in Britain.'

'Sergeant Manning is thinking about sending samples in for analysis.'

'He can go ahead and do that if he wants to waste tax payers' money and make the residents of Mirebury more nervous than they already are.'

'On the other hand, it would restore faith in your meat.'

'I suppose. If that's what he decides to do, then I'll go along with the plan.'

'I think people will be back to eating meat in no time, Jack.'

'I hope so. I couldn't stand living in a town full of vegetarians.'

'Or even worse, people who bought their meat in another town!' Ian added.

Jack gave him a dark look.

'That's not funny.'

'You're right. It's not funny. Who knows? Maybe I'll be the next victim.'

'Somebody bloody well will be, unless we catch this nutter beforehand.'

'I'm going to talk to Jonathan, Simon, Gordon, John, and anybody else who's interested in getting the town watch into action at the market tomorrow morning. We need to launch it tomorrow night.'

'I'll be there, but I'm not waiting until tomorrow. I'm going to start doing rounds tonight.'

'Be careful, Jack. We don't know who we're dealing with.'

'Don't worry about me. But if I catch the fucker, there might be some real human flesh in the streets of Mirebury at daybreak!'

'Call me any time if you need a hand. Any time at all.'

'If I catch sight of him, I won't have time to make phone calls.'

The atmosphere at the Saturday market was heavier than it had ever been in the town's history. There were fewer stalls and customers than usual. Most of the regulars had decided to stay home.

Mary wasn't present. Indeed, she hardly ever left her house

anymore. Her daughter had to force her to go outside at least once a day for a breath of fresh air.

A few people strolled around the market, but they were more occupied looking sideways at each other than in buying produce or chatting happily. Their suspicious thoughts could be read clearly. They were wondering which one of their neighbours was a psychopath hell-bent on destroying Mirebury.

'I've had more fun at funerals than this place,' Ian told Sergeant Manning.

'Nobody seems to be buying or selling,' the sergeant observed. 'It's as though we're all here out of habit without really knowing why.'

'They're here either out of habit or out of defiance. Do you have any news regarding the break-in or the letters?'

'I'm afraid not. There were no clues of any kind at Jack's and the letters were squeaky clean. No witnesses either. Whoever's behind this might be a psychopath, but he sure is a careful one.'

He glanced over Ian's shoulder.

'There's Jack now.'

'Jack, how did it go last night?' Ian asked.

'I didn't see a soul.'

'It doesn't matter. If we keep watch every night, we're bound to catch wind of him eventually.'

Jack's attention was distracted. He was looking around the market boldly.

'Do you see how they're looking at me?'

'Who?'

'Everybody. They keep giving me funny looks. I'm sure they blame me.'

'Rubbish. Nobody blames you for having your shop broken into.'

'Yes, they do.'

Ian looked around, but as much as he wanted to deny it, he had to admit to himself that Jack wasn't being paranoid. He said nothing.

'Ian told me you were thinking about sending some samples of my goods in for analysis, Simon.'

'I was, but if you assure me there's no possibility that the intruder mixed human flesh with your goods, then I won't. I'm not obliged to do so by any regulations if the threat is unfounded.'

'Well, I assure you there's no risk. I check every cut before I wrap it up and hand it to a customer. I know my meat.'

'That's all I wanted to hear, Jack.'

'You don't have any leads at all?'

'No. I've been working on it, but he doesn't leave much of a trail. It's like chasing a phantom.'

'That's why we need to catch him in the act.'

'Here comes Jonathan.'

'Good,' Ian said. 'Gordon should be here shortly too. Maybe John Phelps as well. Then we can get started on working out how to implement the night watch.'

'Good morning, gents,' Jonathan greeted them. 'The Saturday morning market isn't what it used to be.'

'Mirebury's in a sad state, isn't it, Jonathan?'

'Like never before. I hope we'll be able to sort this out before long.'

'We need to launch a counter-offensive. It's the only way,' Jack added, as though it were as simple as cutting a steak. 'We touched on the idea last week, but it can't wait. It needs to happen now!'

The men nodded in vague agreement.

'There's Mitchell Somers. Maybe he'd be interested in being a part of the watch too. The dogs could prove useful,' Ian suggested.

'It's not the best moment,' Sergeant Manning said. 'He's been going through a rough time with the family recently.'

'A rough time? What do you mean by that?' Jack asked.

'With his daughter, Alison. I'm not quite sure how to put it.'

'She's a little difficult to control,' Jonathan cut in diplomatically. 'I hear she's been spending a lot of time with Art, and we all know what he's like.'

'That's about it,' the sergeant said, watching his friend wander around the market with Drover. 'He has enough on his plate with her.'

'How about we go to the pub and talk about what to do?' Jonathan suggested.

'We're waiting for Gordon.'

'I'll give him a call and he can meet us over there.'

'All right. Let's go,' Jack said. 'I think we could all do with a pint. Hopefully, the atmosphere will be a little more hospitable at Harry's.'

'I hope so too,' Sergeant Manning said. 'If we can't feel at ease at The Owl and Moon, then Mirebury really is doomed.'

'When we go home later, we'll probably all find letters telling us not to drink Harry Newcombe's beer because it has urine in it!' Ian joked, determined not to lose his sense of humour.

But nobody laughed.

17

The chill wind had grown stronger by the time Sergeant Manning had wrapped himself up in his warmest coat and donned his leather gloves. He wasn't wearing his police uniform, because he needed to remain as discreet as possible. The only way to catch a shadow is to become one, he figured.

The night was going to be long and the wind sweeping through Mirebury wasn't going to show the young policeman any mercy. He'd just have to grit his teeth and get on with the job. He tried to be optimistic, telling himself that the wind was a meteorological gift from a strategic point of view. It cleaned the streets of the fog that would have otherwise provided the Postman with cover.

It was just after ten o'clock when he began circulating around the streets. His sneakers allowed him to walk quickly without making much noise, and the wind helped smother what little sound he might accidentally make. He pulled his black scarf up around his face.

The streets of Mirebury were poorly lit at night, but the sergeant advanced cautiously, making sure to avoid walking anywhere what little light there was might expose him to watching eyes. Subterfuge was of the utmost importance. After all, he wasn't walking the beat. He was hunting. His aim was not to dissuade, but to apprehend. He made his way slowly towards the church, not for any particular reason, but since he had no idea where the next target might be, it seemed as good a place as any. It also placed him centrally, so that if anybody called his phone, which he'd put on silent mode, he would be able to act quickly.

As he turned a corner, he thought he detected a movement in the sparse foliage of one of the trees lining the pavement. He froze in his tracks. He told himself he'd been mistaken. The

Postman wouldn't be climbing trees. It must have been a squirrel or an owl, or just the wind thrashing at the boughs.

He looked around. There were no signs of life other than the steady glow of electric light and the warm flickering light of fires coming from the windows of nearby homes. The other townsfolk were in their living rooms, sheltered from the wind.

He jogged over to the tree and inspected it more closely. Empty. Its twisted branches were flaying in the wind, lashing wildly with each whistling gust. Dry leaves scuttled along the street, scraping and crackling as the wind hurtled them against moss-covered walls and parked cars.

The sergeant adjusted his scarf and walked away from the tree, following the pavement towards the centre of town, telling himself to remain alert without succumbing to paranoia.

The church was proud and solemn, and its bell tower stood defiantly. Neither winter winds nor social troubles affected the tower of ageless stone. In times gone by, such holy places had been safe havens for populations under attack from raiders and invaders. But this onslaught was different in nature. It was insidious and obscure. No physical walls would keep it at bay.

He looked around, squinting against the wind. The only movement at ground level was that of the leaves, scurrying like frightened mice. Over the rooftops, smoke skulked out of chimneys, only to be whisked away into the night. The howl of the wind would be echoing down into living rooms, where residents were watching television or reading before bedtime. Others would be asleep already, even though the lights were still on. They would have left them on out of fear; a fear it was his job to fight against.

The sergeant knew how to box and how to use his baton, although he'd never been required to put these skills to the test. On the rare occasion, he'd had to check for fingerprints and other clues. But this enemy neither came out to do battle nor left traces of his comings and goings. The sergeant wasn't equipped to catch such a shadowy foe. In big towns, CCTV cameras ensured at least a glimpse of any criminal at large in the public sphere, but similar measures had never been deemed necessary in Mirebury.

Even though Jack had angrily stalked the streets the previous night, Sergeant Manning's patrol was the first official night of the watch. He hoped the Postman was out there, creeping around in the darkness, and he hoped he would catch him that very night. He wanted to become Mirebury's hero.

After scrutinising every shadow, he turned his attention to the church bell tower, the stone heart of Mirebury. The wind roared as it danced invisibly around the tower and thrust its way between the battlements.

'That's where I should be,' he said to himself, his voice muffled in his scarf.

From up there, it would be possible to survey the entire town. He just needed his binoculars, which he kept in the glove compartment of his Range Rover. All he had to do was fetch them, then go and find the set of keys to the church that he kept at the police post.

He dashed back through the streets, stopping at home and the police post, and returned to the church in just over ten minutes. He turned the key and pushed the church door open, making it creak in complaint at the unholy disturbance.

The voluminous interior of the church was menacing in the darkness, and for the first time ever, the holy place made him shiver with dread. He pushed the door closed behind him and switched his torch on, but the light had no substantial impact on the gloom. He swept the beam along the pews as he advanced through the nave and ignored the feeling of discomfort as he pointed his torch at the pulpit and altar. He then turned and headed back towards the entrance and opened the side door giving access to the tower.

Walking up the spiral staircase in the middle of the night was an unsettling experience. The sergeant couldn't even remember the last time he had done so during more godly hours. The tower was the reserve of Father Godfrey and the parish bell ringers. He held his torch in one hand and used the other to keep a grip on the rope so he wouldn't lose his footing as he climbed.

It reminded him of a haunted house he'd once paid a few pence to visit as a boy. There were no fake cobwebs or rubber claws to harass him in the church, but unlike the haunted house, he knew the danger was real.

He kept a tight grip on the rope and stayed close to the wall, where the steps were at their widest. The steep ascent through the darkness was dizzying, and the erratic swing and slash of torchlight only amplified the sensation. But it didn't last long. He arrived in the ringing chamber and allowed himself a moment to catch his breath.

The white walls of the chamber augmented the torchlight, exposing the six bell ropes that hung through holes in the ceiling. They were somehow sinister, like sleeping serpents, and the loops at their ends reminded him of nooses. There was a wooden ladder to one side of the chamber, and it lead up to a trapdoor.

The sergeant tucked his torch away, climbed the ladder, and pushed the trapdoor open.

The walls were unpainted in the belfry, and the bells hung darkly before him, suspended from a thick beam. It was hard to believe the reassuring chimes that could be heard throughout the town on Sunday morning came from this shadowy chamber. There was one double-lancet bell opening in each wall, and the wind whistled through these openings and raced around the bells, shrieking eerily. There would be a decent view over Mirebury from here, but the sergeant wanted to get to the very top of the tower so his view would be completely unobstructed. Of course, it wasn't just a matter of practicality. It was also one of pride. Peeping out from the belfry wasn't exactly a dignified way to supervise the town. Standing guard at the battlements, ready to sound the horn, was the way of a true warden.

He patted a pocket. He didn't have a horn, but he had his phone.

He flashed the torch around until it exposed a ladder leading up to the trapdoor giving access to the roof. He then switched it off and put it in his coat, before climbing the ladder.

96

The trapdoor didn't budge at first. He had to push it several times with considerable force before it gave way. When it finally swung up and onto the roof, the sergeant almost lost his footing. It wasn't far to the belfry floor, but it would have hurt, and he certainly couldn't afford to go twisting an ankle just now.

'Get your act together!' he told himself, emerging into the howling night air.

The view from up there was perfect.

He lifted the binoculars to his eyes, and explored the nightscape. He was like God looking down upon his dominion from the heavens. Father Godfrey wouldn't have liked the young sergeant to make such a comparison, but that didn't matter one little bit. After all, Father Godfrey didn't even know that his church was being used for police business at that very moment. He was probably reading Bible passages or in bed enjoying the sleep of the just while the sergeant was out there doing his bit against flesh and blood evil.

He scanned the town. To his left was the park where the Saturday market was held, and not far from it was Harry Newcombe's pub, about the only place in town that still showed any signs of human life at that late hour. Nothing could scare Harry's weekend regulars away.

In front of him, beyond the houses that included those of Mrs Hopkins and Ian, he could just make out the Mirebury cemetery. It would be blowing a gale over there as well, the wind making a diabolical harmonica of the headstones.

He took a few steps across the bell tower roof, bracing himself against the buffeting wind. He could see the school where the children of Mirebury went each day. It was as dead as the rest of the town, just a couple of shadowy buildings cradled in front of a football field.

There was no sign of the dreaded Postman anywhere.

'Where are you?' the sergeant whispered, but his voice was muffled by his scarf even before the whistling wind had a chance to smother it.

He continued scanning with his binoculars but also looked

down around the centre of town without them from time to time, just in case somebody was moving nearby.

When his feet started to get tired, he sat down, leaning against the battlements. His watch told him it was just after midnight. He was supposed to stay on duty until five o'clock. He closed his eyes for a moment. There was no point in staring at the empty streets for hours on end. A few minutes of rest wouldn't change anything.

Voices woke the sergeant from his sleep and he immediately felt ashamed of himself. He'd only wanted to shut his eyes for a minute or two. He pulled his layers of sleeves back so he could read his watch.

Five past one. He'd been asleep for about forty-five minutes. Not all that long, he told himself.

'But long enough for trouble to be made,' his lips mouthed in admonition.

Despite the wind, which hadn't shown any signs of abating all night, he could hear voices coming from nearby.

He pushed himself to his feet and looked down around the base of the church. He couldn't see anybody, but he could hear the voices. It almost sounded like singing.

But who would be singing outside in the middle of the night?

Or maybe the voices were coming from inside the church, as unlikely as that seemed.

A movement caught his eye. It was a rhythmic movement like the pendulum of a grandfather clock. It came from the old graveyard just behind the church. It was from there that the voices rose against the wailing wind. Two voices chanting some strange song together.

Despite their proximity, the sergeant couldn't make out who was down there, or what they were doing. Had Mirebury been invaded by some kind of pagan cult; worshipping the dead with song and dance?

Once he'd raised his binoculars to his eyes and focused them on the forms in the graveyard below, he discovered just what kind of song and dance was being performed.

He didn't recognise the young man, but the dyed red hair was unmistakable. His friend's seventeen-year-old daughter had been making a habit of roaming the streets at night. He didn't know why Mitchell allowed it. He needed to be stricter with her. But this was more than just staying out late and smoking a joint. He was used to turning a blind eye to the youngsters doing that, off the record, naturally. This was altogether different. Cherry was on all fours between the ancient, moss-covered headstones, and the young man was kneeling in carnal worship behind her. Even though they were dressed warmly in long coats, there was no uncertainty as to what they were doing. Her coat was scrunched up on her back and his hands had a tight grip on her hips. Her two perfect white mounds were being thrust at savagely by the man's groin. They were at it like dogs on heat in the churchyard.

Father Godfrey would most certainly not have approved.

The sergeant was stunned. He wanted to call out to them to stop before he arrested them both for public indecency, but he held his tongue. He didn't want to make things complicated with Mitchell, even if his friend needed a kick up the arse, and, more importantly, he didn't want to give his position away. He had more important matters to concentrate on.

He continued watching the couple through his binoculars, unable to force himself to turn his attention back to scanning the streets of Mirebury. The effect it had on him was unacceptable. His excitement made him feel dirty. But more than that, the fact it was Mitchell's daughter made him feel like the lowest of perverts.

He tried to stop watching, but couldn't. He just couldn't look away as the man rammed himself increasingly rapidly and forcefully between Cherry's creamy buttocks. There wasn't long to go.

The slapping of skin against skin accelerated and then ceased. The man groaned contentedly and withdrew.

'Shit! Who's that?' Cherry called out, almost breathlessly.

The sergeant heard her clearly and was sure his heart skipped a beat, but he quickly realised she wasn't referring to him. She was pointing towards the street that led south from the church.

He followed with his binoculars, but it was already too late, whomever Cherry Somers had seen had already disappeared into the shadows of the night.

She said something that the sergeant couldn't quite make out, but he thought he heard the word *camera*.

The young man pulled his trousers up, zipped his fly closed, and sprang to his feet. He weaved his way through the headstones like one of Mitchell's sheepdogs through an obstacle course, and leaped over the low stone wall that separated the churchyard from the street.

Sergeant Manning was about to start his descent from the tower when he saw that the man had already given up chasing the shadow. He turned back to Cherry and shook his head.

It was too late.

'Was that him?' the sergeant asked himself. But he knew his question would go unanswered, at least for the time being.

'Let's get out of here,' the man said to Cherry as he lit a cigarette, his lighter's flame appearing enormous against the surrounding gloom.

Her head bobbed up and down in agreement.

He put his arm around her, and as they walked off into the distance, he spoke inaudible words and seemed to be laughing.

Cherry turned her head around as though looking behind her and lifted the tail of her coat.

'That's disgusting!' she complained loudly, slapping his face.

The sergeant shook his head in disbelief before turning his binoculars back to where the voyeur had been spotted. There was nothing but impenetrable darkness.

18

Brett Greyson milked his cows before dawn, just like he did every day without fail. Once he was done in the milking shed, he would head back to the cottage to have a hearty breakfast of sausages, hash browns, beans, and a couple of eggs sprinkled with salt and pepper. Living a bit out of town gave the Greysons a sense of safety. They were happy to be further away from the growing unease plaguing Mirebury. Brett slaughtered his own animals, so he knew exactly what was on his plate on any given day. There was no chance he had unwittingly devoured human flesh. When he went into town, he could feel the mistrust in the air. Suspicious looks were exchanged when paths crossed and people were constantly looking over their shoulders. Otherwise minor differences of opinion and petty disputes between residents were coming to the surface like dead fish. Trivial problems were becoming tense standoffs. He preferred to stay on the farm with his family, well away from all that bother.

'I'm going into town to get my hair done this morning, Brett.'

'All right, love, but don't get yourself caught up in all that trouble that's going on, will you?' he mumbled through a mouthful of egg.

'Don't worry. You know I don't like gossip. Do you need anything while I'm there?'

'Just the local rag.'

'You big hypocrite! And you talk to me about steering clear of gossip.'

'You're probably right. All the same, I like to keep track of the news.'

Brett finished his breakfast and cleared the table.

'Up and at 'em. I've got to fix the bottom paddock fence today.'

He gave his wife a peck on the cheek.

'Have fun in town, and don't forget my paper.'

'I won't. Now go and fix that fence before the girls get loose and the neighbours come around to complain.'

'You're a slave driver, just like your mother, but I love you all the same.'

She smiled as she raised her left hand and imitated giving him a good whipping.

Mitchell Somers's house was towards the end of George's round. He had what looked like a bill for Mirebury's top shepherd. Most of his deliveries were bills, since very few people still sent each other personal letters—Mrs Hopkins being the only resident who sent and received correspondence on a weekly basis.

He brought his bicycle to a stop at the Somers's letterbox and checked inside. He was about to drop the bill into it when he noticed there was already another envelope waiting to be collected. That struck him as unusual because he hadn't delivered any mail to them in several days and was quite sure Mitchell or Jenny checked every morning without fail. One of them was often out front when he passed by and said hello.

He picked the envelope up carefully between his thumb and index finger as though expecting it to explode in his face.

But it didn't.

It was plain and unstamped. No name or address. He turned it over to see if there was a sender's address on the back, but there wasn't. It wasn't sealed either. He tried to resist, reminding himself that he'd never once broken the sacred code, but this was different. Times were changing and rules didn't seem to make much sense now. The temptation was simply too great. He had to look inside.

He pulled the flap out and withdrew the envelope's contents, then sucked in a deep breath as his eyes widened. Never before had he seen an image like the one shown in the photograph.

He looked around, afraid that somebody might be watching him and reading his thoughts on his face.

His fingers held the picture nervously.

George's first reaction had been one of shock, but it was quickly replaced by the sad notion that an erotic ingredient had been missing from his bland life all these years. He found himself glancing guiltily at the photograph again.

What he saw was absolutely shocking. He'd never even imagined doing to his wife what Brett Greyson was doing to Cherry Somers in that picture.

He adjusted the front of his trousers and tried to clear his mind, but there were so many questions. What was Brett doing with a girl young enough to be his daughter? Why was she letting him do *that* to her? And the most disturbing and perplexing question of all was what to do with the letter.

He looked towards the Somers's house. Everyone in town knew Cherry was a bit of a wild child, but who would have expected her to be involved in such a decadent liaison with a down-to-earth, god-fearing, and supposedly happily married dairy farmer?

The photograph was burning his hand like hot coals. Part of him wanted to keep it, but he told himself he needed to get rid of it. The most responsible action to take would be to throw it away where nobody would ever find it. On the other hand, perhaps he had a moral obligation to knock on the door and show Mitchell what kind of disgusting sexual games his teenage daughter was being caught up in, or, more likely, instigating. After all, there was no doubt she was the one teaching Greyson the rules of the game.

The decision was too difficult to make, so George decided not to make it at all. He would pretend he hadn't noticed the letter in the first place. It would be as simple as that.

He slipped the explicit photograph back into the envelope and dropped it back into the letterbox, making sure the bills he had to deliver lay on top. He looked helplessly at the Somers's house and pedalled away.

19

Later that morning, after he'd repaired the fence and was walking back to his tool shed, a Range Rover came roaring along Brett Greyson's drive. He froze in his tracks, staring in bewilderment, and was getting ready to leap aside. But the vehicle skidded to a halt in front of him.

He could see Mitchell Somers behind the wheel and Drover in the passenger seat. Mitchell was clearly furious.

Brett cast a coil of wire and pliers to the ground near the shed door and found himself absentmindedly wiping his hands on his grey coveralls as he frowned questioningly at the unexpected visitor.

'You filthy pervert! How dare you!' Mitchell yelled as he burst out of his Range Rover and waved an axe handle over his head. Drover was at his side, barking in unison with his master's fanfare of insults.

'Slow down there, Mitchell! What the hell are you on about?' Brett snapped back at him defensively.

'Don't give me that! You know very well!'

'Listen Mitchell, how about you just get right off my property now. I don't take kindly to being spoken to like this.'

The men had their differences, and harsh words had been exchanged in the past, but Brett had never seen Mitchell this angry before. It scared the hell out of him, but he refused to back down. He had to stand his ground.

'What about *my* property, you filthy pig? You were all over *that*!'

Mitchell kept marching towards his target, the axe handle still raised.

Brett decided to change tact. If defence wasn't going to dissuade Mitchell from his fit of insanity, maybe humour would make him snap out of it.

'Mitchell, you've lost the plot, good man. Have you been eating mushrooms from the woods near Damian Granger's caravan?'

'Don't get smart with me!' he spat

Drover joined in, barking at the hunted man, faithful to his master without understanding what it was all about.

'I just want to know what's got into you, Mitchell.'

Brett backed away as Mitchell drew closer. He'd thought the axe handle was a prop at first, that Mitchell had brought it for no other reason than to show that he was angry and wanted to be taken seriously. Looking the man in the eye, it was now clear he intended to use it.

'Don't give me that, Brett. Be man enough to admit to your actions.'

'Keep back, Mitchell,' Brett growled at him like a cornered dog. 'I'm doing my best to be patient with you because I can see you aren't yourself, but you need to stop right now and put the axe handle down.'

Mitchell ignored him.

'I'm warning you!'

'Warning *me*! You're threatening *me*! I'll kill you!'

Brett looked around in panic, then dashed into his shed.

'No use trying to hide, you dirty coward!'

Mitchell marched over to the shed. He had his man cornered.

'Get off my property, you madman!' Brett's voice, fearful and angry, boomed from within.

Mitchell stopped dead in his tracks, suddenly less aggressive, but Drover kept growling and snapping. He backed away from the shed, and Brett reappeared, brandishing a shotgun.

'You're going to shoot me then, are you? Is that what it's come to?'

'I'm telling you, Mitchell. You need to leave. You've obviously lost it. You're raving mad, but if there's even a glimmer of sense still left in that thick head of yours, you'd better listen to it and piss off right now.'

'You don't have the balls!' Mitchell hissed, pointing at Brett's groin with his axe handle.

Brett raised his shotgun and looked along the barrel at Mitchell.

'Keep back. I'll defend myself if I need to. I *do* have the balls!'

'All your balls are good for is corrupting good men's daughters! It's your fault how she's become!'

Mitchell raised the axe handle and lunged forward. 'You'll pay for that!'

Both men were equally startled by the deafening blast.

Mitchell froze in his tracks, not understanding why he didn't feel any pain and hadn't been knocked to the ground.

Brett was shocked as well, his gaze fixed at Mitchell's feet.

Mitchell followed his gaze down.

His prize dog was twitching in a pool of blood. The twitching soon stopped.

'Drover!'

Mitchell's gaze sprang back to Brett.

'You bastard!'

He took one great stride forward and his axe handle came crashing down, striking Brett's head with a dull thud. He swung again, and it happened so easily, almost automatically. His rage did the work for him. Brett now lay motionless at his feet, but the axe handle kept slamming into his head. Mitchell felt like an eager onlooker. With every swing, every thud or crack, a wave of anger dissipated. After half a dozen blows, he dropped the weapon and turned to Drover.

'Come on, boy!'

The dog didn't react.

'Come on, Drover. Get up, boy'

Mitchell wasn't in any state of mind to accept reality. His rage had subsided and he was now strangely calm. He took his dog in his arms, ignoring the blood that soaked its coat, and carried it back to the Range Rover, whispering comforting words.

20

The following day, Mirebury was a ghost town. The news was received with a shocked disbelief that gradually developed into a sense of hopelessness. The details of what had happened were unclear, but three certainties were evident and had rapidly become public knowledge. Brett Greyson had been bashed to death, Mitchell Somers had been reported missing, and Mrs Somers had found a photo in her husband's underwear drawer showing a repulsive sex act that she 'could never have imagined physically possible' involving Brett Greyson and her teenage daughter.

Sergeant Manning dreaded the task that lay ahead, but there was no avoiding it. He had to interview Mrs Somers and Mrs Greyson, the wives of two of his closest friends. They were at their respective homes, surrounded by friends and family who were trying to comfort them and understand exactly what had happened.

The policeman's hands were sweating and he felt ill. He took a deep breath and wiped his hands on his trousers before pressing Mrs Greyson's doorbell. The shrill ding-dong echoed inside the house, starkly discordant with the heavy atmosphere. She answered the door herself and the sergeant's brave face almost cracked when he saw how dazed she looked. Her eyes were bleary and her cheeks streaked. Her world had been turned upside down and all sense shaken out of it. She put a hand against the doorframe to keep herself from losing her balance.

'Sit down, Mrs Greyson,' he instructed her, removing his cap with one hand and ushering her back to the living room with the other.

Her brow furrowed for an instant, but she quickly understood why he'd chosen not to address her by her first name. It was for his benefit as much as for hers. He was on duty and had to remain professional about the whole affair. There was a time and place for tears.

'Thank you,' she whispered, and asked the others present to give the two of them some privacy for a while.

Once they were alone, she asked Sergeant Manning to pour some tea, and they sat and sipped in silence while he gathered his thoughts.

'We'll find Mitchell Somers,' he began, doing his best to keep his words calm and composed. 'And we'll make sure he's held accountable for what he has done. At this stage, I can't make head nor tail of it, but if murder has been committed, I have to put all personal feelings aside and do my job.'

She listened but was too shocked to respond. She was still coming to terms with the horrible reality of the situation, that the only man she had ever known, who had accompanied her as she grew from a shy girl to a confident woman, and had fathered her children, was now gone, bludgeoned to death. She was numb and confused. The rules of the game of life had been infringed and the umpire was nowhere to be found.

He went to the kitchen to speak to her friends and family, hoping to gain even the slightest insight, but there was nothing to be discovered. They were all adamant that Brett had never touched Cherry. The idea was ridiculous.

He took his leave, promising to keep them informed, and drove to the home of the Somers family. Mrs Somers was in much the same state, except that she didn't know if her husband was dead or alive. She'd never known him to be a violent man, but she showed the photo to the sergeant as a way of explaining why he'd gone berserk.

The sergeant cringed. He wasn't a father, but he'd known Alison all her life, and what he saw made him upset. He pushed his feelings aside. There was no room for emotion in a criminal investigation. A homicide squad would soon arrive in Mirebury to take the matter out of his inexperienced hands, but he wanted to have something to impress them with.

'I have to ask you a few questions, Mrs Somers. Have you spoken to your daughter about this?'

She was understandably embarrassed.

'Do stop with all this *Mrs Somers* business, Simon.'

He closed his eyes, hoping to escape the reality of what was happening, but when he opened them again the same shattered face was there in front of him, begging him to make everything all right. Only, he couldn't make it all right. One friend was dead, his head bashed open like a piñata by another, who was now a fugitive. There could be no happy conclusion to the affair, and there wasn't a soul in Mirebury who didn't know it.

'Please understand that I need to maintain a degree of distance. It's not to be cruel to you, but to protect both of us.'

'I guess you're right. Alison has locked herself in her room and won't speak to anybody. All she told me was that Brett never touched her and that she has no idea where the photo came from. She swears it's not real, and I believe her.'

'Not real?'

'She insists he's never touched her. The photo must have been...what's the word?'

'I know what you mean; photoshopped.'

'Exactly.'

'I'll need to keep it for analysis.'

She frowned.

'It's evidence.'

'Of course,' she said.

'Did you receive it by mail?'

'I found it in Mitchell's sock drawer. I don't know where he got it from. Do you think this is related to all the horrible business that's been going on recently?'

'I don't know, but it seems possible. I've got the feeling we're all being played like puppets.'

He carefully bagged the photograph, even though he doubted there would be any fingerprints on it other than those of Mitchell and Jenny Somers.

'Mrs Somers, think carefully before answering this question.'

She shook her head slowly but with determination before he could pose it.

'No, Sergeant Manning. I have *no* idea where Mitchell is,' she managed to say before breaking down.

The triple blow of learning that her husband had just committed the greatest mistake of his life, that he was now a fugitive, and that she was condemned to live the rest of her life in shame had destroyed the poor woman. She wanted to speak to the Greysons, to tell them it was all just a misunderstanding and that the photograph was a fake. But what could she possibly say to a family that had just lost its father? A *mistake*, a *fake photograph*, it was absurd. What difference could any of that make to them? Brett was dead. It was easy to blame the so-called Postman, but her husband was the one who had smashed Brett's skull to bits with an axe handle.

'I'm sorry,' Sergeant Manning reticently interrupted her train of thought. 'I have to go now. You understand? Your friends will look after you until a counsellor arrives from the city. Try to get Alison to leave her room. She must feel terribly upset about what has happened. Tell her you know it's not real, that she has become the victim of a cruel game; just like Mrs Hopkins and Jack Fuller. It's not her fault. I need to find Mitchell, but I also need to find whoever is behind all this. I will find him, Mrs Somers. Mirebury will not be torn apart.'

She stared him in the eye, making contact with the friend behind the uniform.

'Simon, darling, let's be frank—it's already too late.'

21

In the wake of what had happened between Brett and Mitchell, many of the townsfolk found themselves taking sides. For some, the photograph was real and Mitchell had reacted the way any loving father would. It was manslaughter at worst and he deserved to be pardoned. For others, the photograph was a fake and Brett had been murdered in cold blood by a man who shouldn't have been so naive.

Alison refused to leave her room, much to the disappointment of those who wanted the little harlot to set the record straight once and for all.

In an attempt to counter the divisiveness that was infecting the town, Father Godfrey decided to open the church every night. It would be the town's place of refuge, where residents could come to pray and talk. He was convinced the devil had come to Mirebury to test their faith, and, judging by what was happening, they were all failing.

The bulletin board outside the church announced his plan of action:

This sanctuary will be open every night from nine o'clock until dawn. I urge you to come to pray, sing, dance, and most importantly of all, talk together. In this time of darkness, we must stay united and trust the Lord, our Saviour!

Father Godfrey went to the town hall, the pub, and the school to promote his initiative. It was imperative that the whole of Mirebury be aware of his strategy.

What he detected in these places worried him greatly. Evil was at large. It was all around them. There were daggers in the eyes of his fellow man and trouble brewing in their hearts. Neighbour suspected neighbour and everyone was afraid he or she would be the next to be accused. If a decent man like Mitchell Somers could be tricked into committing murder, what hope was there for the rest of them? The task of convincing his flock to remain sheep, and not become wolves, was going to be the greatest challenge of Father Godfrey's career. It was an unwelcome challenge, but he took it upon himself with determination and a sense of duty. Mirebury was balancing on a cliff edge, and the slightest gust would send the town over the brink.

He was ready to work hard. There was so much to be done. There would be little sleep at night with the church being kept open. People relied on him to comfort and guide them, and there was a funeral to organise.

'How are you, Charlotte?'

The look she gave Ian was searching. She wanted to know whether he was merely extending a prescribed greeting or sincerely enquiring about her wellbeing. She hoped it was the latter, and that he truly cared how she felt. The way he'd asked her had been straightforward and frank, but she had the impression he wasn't the type to overstate, so perhaps he really was interested in hearing her concerns. It mattered a great deal to her.

'How are you coping? Do tell me.'

She breathed a sigh of relief.

'To be honest, I'm a little disturbed. Is it always like this here?'

'It really isn't. I promise you Mirebury hasn't always been like this. Quite the contrary. None of this makes any sense to any of us. Don't give up on the town yet. It's going through a rough patch and we need to fight.'

'A rough patch? That's rather diplomatic of you. It's more than that, and I'm more than a little disturbed. I'm scared, Ian. I'm not ashamed to admit that. You seem to be the only sane person here.'

'I'm scared too. We all are. But we're going to fight back, aren't we? We need to pull together and support each other.'

'I agree with you, absolutely. I don't want to give up on Mirebury. I don't want to run off without a fight. That's not the kind of person I am. But it's not safe here.'

'No. It's not safe at the moment. We can't lie to ourselves about that. We need to do the best we can to ensure our safety without giving in to fear and panic. I think you should stay with me tonight, Charlotte. It would be safer for you.'

Despite her heavy heart, she managed to laugh.

'I thought you were an honourable gentleman, not the kind to take advantage of a damsel in distress,' she teased.

'I would never take advantage of a vulnerable young woman, but, I must admit, I'm not as respectable as I may have led you to believe.'

The corners of her mouth twitched. She was pleased to discover this side of Ian.

'Well, in that case, I accept your offer. Thank you. When should I come over?'

'Come whenever you like. If I'm not at home, I'll be across the road with Mrs Hopkins.'

'Taking advantage of her and all?'

'A librarian with an inappropriate sense of humour,' he mused. 'I like it. See you later.'

But later came sooner than Ian expected. There were three measured knocks at the door, evenly spaced. He could tell she was trying to hide her eagerness. He took a deep breath and let it out slowly.

'Come inside, Charlotte.'

The table was set; his best dishes, silver cutlery, flowers, candles, and champagne.

She smiled to herself and tried not to blush.

'This is very impressive, Ian. Should I feel flattered or is this how you treat all your guests?'

'Feel free to be flattered. Tonight, I want to forget about all the problems around us. Jack is keeping watch, and if *he* can't keep our streets safe, nobody can, not even Simon. I want to relax. We both deserve it, and we both need it.'

She turned her head and pretended to be inspecting the rest of the room, but she was biting her bottom lip and holding her breath. Once she'd regained her composure, she turned back to him with her most delightful smile and was sure she noticed his knees buckle ever so slightly.

'So, you think I can help you forget about what's happening outside?' she asked casually.

'I know you can.'

He put some background music on and popped the cork on the champagne.

'You're quite the talk of the town at the moment, you know?'

'Am I now? And what does the town say about me?'

'They say you're mysterious,' he told her as he carefully filled two champagne flutes. He was more accustomed to pint glasses.

'Do they really? I don't feel very mysterious. I wonder how I gave them that impression.'

Ian handed her one of the glasses.

'I don't know, but I agree with them.'

She gave him the most theatrically enigmatic look she could manage, with eyes narrowed and chin clasped ponderingly between index finger and thumb.

They laughed.

'To mystery,' Ian toasted, raising his glass to meet hers.

They sipped.

'Maybe you're the mysterious one?' her glistening lips said.

'Me? You're joking, aren't you?'

'No. For example, why did you leave London to come here? That seems strange.'

'Not really. I've never felt I belonged in the city. I was offered a job here, thought I'd give it a go, and ended up falling in love with the place. It's as simple as that. What about you? Where are you from then? You sound like a west country girl.'

'I'm from Bristol, actually. There's no mystery in leaving Bristol for a charming village.'

Charming indeed, she reminded herself, but chased the negative thoughts from her mind. Instead, she sipped at the champagne and let the bubbles tickle her tongue and cheeks.

'This is your first time away from home?'

'Not at all. I've travelled and worked in far stranger parts of the world than here. I've taught English in China and Vietnam, and I lived in Austria for a couple of years.'

'There you go. You *are* mysterious after all.'

She laughed.

'Why did you live in Austria? Did you teach English there too?'

'No, I worked in a Kaffeehaus. I went there with an Austrian boyfriend I met through friends in Bristol and, well, stayed with him until I found him playing around with a Russian girl one day when I came home from work early.'

'I'd say he had a thing for foreign girls.'

'So it seemed. What about you, Ian?'

'Well, I don't think so. No, not really. Although, I've always wanted to try a Japanese girl.'

She pretended to be shocked.

'No, you pervert. I mean why don't you tell me a little about *you* now?'

'Of course you did. How silly of me.'

'*Try* a Japanese girl? A woman's not a shoe, Ian.'

He laughed and was going to make a comment about being walked all over but thought better of it.

'Well, I grew up in London, where most of my family still lives, and I thought I was happy enough there until I came here. I guess I'm a country lad at heart but never had the chance to learn that about myself before.'

'Have you broken the hearts of any of the women here?'

'No, I shouldn't think so. At least, none that still live here.'

'You don't seem like a heartbreaker.'

'Is that a compliment?'

'Of course it is.'

'In that case, thank you.'

He refilled her glass.

'Don't get me drunk before dinner.'

'Talking about dinner, it should be ready soon. Will you do me the honour of accompanying me to the table?'

'With pleasure,' she said, raising her hand with befitting theatrical elegance.

Ian poured two glasses of Pauillac from the bottle he'd opened and left to decant before her arrival and lit the candles. He then disappeared into the kitchen, leaving Charlotte to admire all the effort he'd gone to. Unaccustomed as he was to hosting romantic dinners, he enjoyed preparing and eating good food, even if only for one. He'd guessed it wasn't that difficult to do the same for two, with a little added attention to detail. He knew trends were forever changing, and that the dating game was undoubtedly constantly evolving, but he figured that beyond fads like Tinder and "Netflicks and chill", you could never go wrong with cooking a fine meal and sharing it by candlelight. The art of true romance would never become uncool. It was an eternal part of human interaction, wasn't it? He certainly hoped so.

The glint in Charlotte's eyes and flicker on her lips when he came back wasn't just from the play of candlelight on her face. He knew she was suitably impressed.

'I absolutely love shepherd's pie,' she told him. 'Jack's finest lamb?'

'He promised me it was.'

He watched as she raised a forkful to her mouth and savoured it.

'Delicious,' she confirmed.

'You won't miss your family and friends in Bristol?' he asked.

Charlotte looked at him thoughtfully. She finished her mouthful and took a sip of wine before replying.

'It's a long story, and one I'd rather not share with you just yet. Relax. There's no need to look so concerned. It's not as bad as I'm probably making it sound. My parents' marriage wasn't the most harmonious. That's what it boils down to. The only time they really got along was when they were reading. They would sit in silence and lose themselves in a book. They passed that passion on to me.'

'I didn't mean to pry.'

'It's fine. I'm an only child, but I have cousins around the country, and friends all over the world. My closest friends are home in Bristol.'

'It's not hard being away from them? It was tough for me at first. It doesn't matter that I chose to come here. It was a big change and it wasn't easy being accepted. Most of the locals welcomed me and were friendly enough, but I'll always be the newcomer.'

'That's *my* title now,' she corrected him.

He found himself gazing at her wistfully, then sipped at his wine to hide his embarrassment.

'I really do hope this rough patch, as you put it, gets smoothed out, Ian. I want to be happy here. I want this to become my home, where I feel safe and...' She caught herself before that last word escaped her lips.

'It will, Charlotte. Mirebury is going to get through this. I swear you'll feel safe. I hope you already do here with me tonight.'

He noticed a faint shiver flow through her.

'I do. I haven't felt safer in a long time.'

'Are you ready for dessert?' he asked, noticing that she'd finished her shepherd's pie and eager to change the topic of conversation.

She smiled and said yes with her eyes.

Ian disappeared into the kitchen and returned carrying a tray with two crystal bowls and silver spoons in one hand and the bottle of champagne which he'd put back in the fridge before dinner in the other.

'Chocolate mousse? Did you make it yourself?'

He nodded.

'You see, you are quite the man of mystery after all. Do you have other hidden talents?'

'A few that are hidden even to me, I'm sure.'

He served the desserts and poured champagne.

'Can we eat them on the sofa?' Charlotte asked.

'That's an excellent idea. We'd be much more comfortable.'

She slipped her shoes off and placed them by the front door, then sat up against one arm of the sofa with her legs crossed.

Ian followed suit, amazed at how comfortable they were together, and at how similar they seemed to be. He hoped he wouldn't end up making a mess of it.

'Your mousse is delicious, Ian. It truly is.' As if to prove she meant it, she took another scoop and put it in her mouth, then pulled the spoon out between closed lips.

'Thank you,' he said, looking from her chocolate smeared lips to her green eyes.

'I want to know more about you, Ian,' she said. 'I want you to share a secret with me.'

He understood the meaning behind her words. It wasn't just playful flirting. She felt at ease with him, just as he did with her. That was obvious. But she needed to be sure. She needed more. She was asking him to trust her, to bare himself to her.

'What do you want to know?'

She sipped her champagne.

'I want to know what you fear. I'm not talking about what's going on out there. I mean in general.'

He drank his champagne thoughtfully.

'You'll think it's silly,' he said.

'That doesn't matter. I want to know you; both the serious you, and the silly you.'

'When I was a teenager, I used to dream I'd gone to school without my trousers and pants. I had my shirt and tie, but was naked from the waist down.'

Charlotte laughed. 'And you still have this dream?'

'Not now. But I'm still a bit prudish in public. I don't even like taking my shirt off at the beach.'

'But it's only a problem in public?'

'Only in public.'

'That's good to hear.'

'What about you?' he asked, trying to keep a straight face.

118

'Me? I'm a bit claustrophobic. I don't like using lifts or travelling through tunnels.'

'Not an issue in Mirebury,' he said. 'We don't have either of those things anywhere in town as far as I know.'

'It's my turn now.'

She nodded.

'Do you have a secret desire?'

She thought for a while.

'You know, I don't think so. I want to be happy. That's all. I enjoy my work. I guess I want what most people do, a happy home, and a family.'

She looked at him questioningly. 'And you?'

'The same,' he said, holding her gaze. 'The same.'

'And to try a Japanese girl?'

They laughed.

'It's not a priority. I swear. I just want to be loved, and to have a family of my own. I also want to get closer to nature. I've already achieved that by leaving the city, but I want to go further. I've been here for six years already, but I don't know the surrounding moors all that well.'

'Not quite the master yet? Hey, maybe we could discover them together,' she whispered. 'I'd like that.'

He poured the last few drops of champagne and they drank it. They had moved closer to each other during their conversation, without really being aware of it, and once they had drained their glasses, they kissed passionately. They revelled in the taste of chocolate and champagne on each other's tongues, and their hands began to wander and explore.

Neither was really aware who had instigated the move, but they drifted from the sofa to the bedroom, still entwined in perfect union. There was no shyness or sense of self-awareness. After all, they weren't children and they both knew what they wanted.

Ian was afraid he would be out of practice, but his lengthy celibacy had served to make him more passionate than ever. He took her clothes off and undid her bra. He hadn't forgotten how to do that. He kissed her all over, the taste of her body and perfume mixing with the sweetness in his mouth. His tongue caressed her rosy nipples and he let a curious hand slide down her back and between her buttocks.

Afterwards, the librarian slid gracefully out of the bed and reached into her toiletry bag, letting Ian admire her milky body, which glowed under the soft light of his bedside lamp. She then threw a blanket around her shoulders and stepped across to the bedroom window.

'I didn't know you smoked,' he said, doing his best not to sound disappointed.

'Only on special occasions.'

'Is that a fact?'

She smiled at him as she brought the lighter up to her mouth.

'Don't let Mrs Hopkins see you, for heaven's sake,' he begged. *'So Ian, I see you've found a lady friend, and I couldn't help but notice she likes to smoke naked at windows.'*

They laughed.

'Oh!' Charlotte stepped back quickly, looking panicked.

'What is it?'

She hid behind a curtain and gazed into the dark street like a mouse observing a hungry cat from its hiding place. The fog had risen a little, affording a clearer view.

'What's wrong? Is it the Postman?' Ian was already out of bed and stumbling towards the window.

'I don't know who it is, but he's got a meat cleaver!'

Ian burst out laughing, but it soon collapsed into a groan. His relief was mixed with disappointment.

'That's Jack, our local butcher. He's on night duty. You haven't met him yet?'

'No,' Charlotte answered, remaining hidden. She didn't want the butcher to see her stripped down to the bone. 'I'm trying to cut back on red meat. The whole industry disgusts me, to be honest.'

'Whatever you do, don't repeat what you just said in front of him!'

'There's no chance of that. I've just one question, Ian. Is it part of the plan for whoever happens to be on night duty to walk around with sharp utensils?'

'Jack does things his way, and with what's been happening lately, Sergeant Manning isn't likely to arrest him for going armed in public.'

Jack was walking slowly along the street, looking all about with a theatrical display of vigilance. His meat cleaver rested impatiently against his broad shoulder, ready to strike out. The disgraced butcher was just begging to take a hooded man on a creaky bicycle by surprise.

'Give me a minute, Charlotte. I want to see how he's going. I feel guilty in here, enjoying the company of an angel while he patrols the cold streets.'

'You think I'm an angel, after what we just did?'

'Well, maybe a fallen angel.'

She laughed from her hiding place.

'Go on, but be quick about it. Shall I pour you a brandy?'

'Please. That's how I like to celebrate special occasions,' he said, pulling his trousers on. 'There's a bottle of cognac in the drinks cabinet.'

He hurried outside and called softly through the fog so Jack would know he was approaching, figuring it was best not to startle the armed watchman.

'Jack! It's me. It's Ian.'

'Ian? Hello. I was thinking of dropping in to see you, but it would have been too tempting to stay inside. You haven't seen or heard the old bicycle?'

'I haven't noticed anything strange at all. He probably won't strike two nights in a row anyway.'

'I wish he bloody well would. I'm itching to get a hold of the blighter.'

'I know you are, Jack. So am I.'

'This time he's gone too far, Ian. Digging up the remains of a war hero, joking about putting human flesh in my shop, humiliating a teenage girl; all that is outrageous enough, but this time he has blood on his hands. He's made a murderer of a decent man and condemned another to the grave. Worse than that, the hand of death is still looming over Mirebury, and it's going to strike again very soon.'

Ian looked around nervously through the fog and the dark.

'What are you talking about, Jack? What makes you say that?'

'I was talking to Father Godfrey before starting my rounds. He says the townsfolk aren't reacting well to this tragedy. Instead of it uniting them, making them more determined to catch the Postman, they're losing all hope. Mirebury has already been defeated without even putting up a fight. The town is going to tear itself apart before long.

'Quite a number of people are at church as we speak, and Father Godfrey has been listening to their concerns and counselling them. He says that suspicion is staining the town's spirit and that unfounded accusations are rife. Many of the women say their husbands think they know who the Postman is are going to take matters into their own hands. Brett's closest mates, despite his wife's pleas to keep a cool head, have armed themselves to the teeth and are out looking for Mitchell. They couldn't care less about the Postman. All they want is to avenge Brett's death. The police have launched a manhunt and I just hope they find Mitchell before he gets himself killed.'

Jack paused for a moment and rubbed his beard thoughtfully.

'I'm telling you, Ian. I wouldn't be surprised if another resident ends up dead before dawn.'

Ian wondered what he could do. It was hard enough fighting against one maniac, but if the entire town was descending into chaos, Mirebury really was lost. They were playing into his hands. He guessed all he could do was stay home and keep watch over his small corner of town; over Charlotte, beside him in bed, and Mrs Hopkins across the street.

The church bell rang out, reassuring the townsfolk that the Lord's house was open to them. Whether they chose to take shelter there was up to them. But the fact that they had the option was in itself a great comfort. Whatever else happened, it

122

would remain open to them—a safe haven.

'I'm off, Ian. I can't stay here chatting all night.'

'I know, Jack. Listen. Just promise me you'll be careful. I'll have my phone with me all night. Call me if you need backup.'

'I will, Ian.'

The butcher disappeared into the thinning fog as the last chime of the bell faded.

22

The announcement was made at the last minute, but word spread around town like the plague. Mayor Larkins had declared an emergency meeting at the town hall and expected every resident to be there at seven o'clock, and not a minute later. Brett Greyson's death had forced him to take the step he'd been hesitating to take since the moment he realised that the break-in at Jack's butcher shop was related to the desecration of Mr Hopkins's final resting place.

A wolf in sheep's clothing was hidden among them and it had to be hunted down. An organised and united course of action was Mirebury's only hope.

This wolf would quite possibly attend the very meeting that was going to be held in order to find a way to fight it. That couldn't be avoided, and at any rate, the purpose of the assembly was not specifically to attempt to reveal the identity of the Postman but rather to discuss strategies for weakening his hold on the town. If the people of Mirebury could render themselves immune to the Postman's provocations, then he would surely lose interest in his morbid game and disappear from their lives.

As the clocks of Mirebury struck seven o'clock, most of the town's residents arrived at the hall. There was little chatting or idle gossip. Cold glares and sideways glances were the order of the day. The formerly friendly atmosphere was gone. If eyes were daggers, the town hall would have been flowing crimson with blood.

Several people didn't show up at the meeting. Jack was one of them. After keeping guard all night and working the next day, he'd chosen the warm embrace of sleep. His absence encouraged the few residents who suspected him of being the Postman to hold firm to their belief. But his wife and children were there, representing the Fuller family's honour and bearing themselves with pride.

None of the members of the Greyson or Somers families were present either, but that came as no surprise and didn't arouse any suspicion.

Mrs Hopkins had also decided to stay at home, unable to believe that murder had been committed in her quiet town.

Once everybody was seated, Mayor Larkins took the microphone, drew a deep breath, and nodded sadly as he scanned the hall.

'Ladies and gentlemen,' he began. 'First of all, thank you for coming this evening.'

The faces that looked back at him were heavy with a sense of hopelessness. They were relying on him, as their elected leader, to show them the way out of this terrible state of affairs.

'I will not waste our time with empty words. We are all here tonight to discuss the misuse of our good town's letterboxes by an individual whom many of you call the Postman. This person is not to be confused with our trusty employee of the Royal Mail here with us tonight.' He smiled at George.

'Maybe it's him!' Gavin Kemble shouted.

The assembly laughed, but it was hollow, tense laughter.

'Be quiet!' Anne White yelled.

'This is no laughing matter, you fools!' Old Patterson bellowed.

'No, seriously, it *could* be!' Aiden Hart added.

'It could be any one of us!' Art Rekeby yelled. 'We've all got a screw or two loose.'

The hollow laughter echoed again, and the tension was even more palpable than before.

'Let's show the mayor some respect! Hold your tongues!' Helen Sykes, usually elegant and reserved, found herself shouting.

'What are you talking about? Why would I?' George shouted in response to the mechanic's attack, blatantly ignoring Helen. He was incensed.

'You've never liked Mirebury, George. I remember you told me once that you'd have done anything to leave this town,' Gavin went on. He'd never really liked George, for reasons he didn't understand himself, and was just having a go at him, enjoying seeing him squirm like a worm on a hook.

'That was years ago,' George shouted back.

'Yeah, it could be him,' Art piped up again.

'It could be anybody. Why pick on George?' Aiden countered, the two of them now in role reversal. It made no sense, but that hardly mattered. Aiden just wanted to have it out with Art. Like most of the townsfolk, he despised him because of his relationship with Cherry.

The spectacle was beyond ridiculous.

'Seriously though, my bet is Damian Granger,' Art said. 'He wants us to think he's nothing but an eccentric loner out there in his caravan, picking mushrooms and playing the druid, but he's got a few rabbits loose. He's not here tonight, is he?'

'Good point. Where is he?' Gavin asked the gathering.

'Quiet, please!' the mayor shouted, his tone clearly indicating that he wasn't amused at all. 'This is precisely what I want to talk to you about, this unhealthy trend of making groundless accusations and sowing the seeds of suspicion.'

He glared at the assembly until their voices subsided into an equally disturbing quiet.

'This Postman, who may very well be among us tonight...'

The audience began chatting loudly and glancing accusatorily at each other again.

The mayor clapped next to the microphone.

Hands shot up to cover offended ears.

He took a deep breath, recomposed himself, and released a sigh.

'The so-called Postman seems to be playing a game with us, but we are taking measures to catch him, and catch him we will. Several of our fellow residents, to whom I convey my heartfelt gratitude, have been keeping guard over Mirebury at night. Sergeant Manning has been doing all he can to track this madman down and he now has invaluable constabulary backup to make the task more manageable for him. A CID unit is on its way and will be launching an investigation, and I'm sure you will all fully cooperate with the detectives.

'However, what I want to say to you this evening is that we must not simply rely on these attempts to catch the Postman red-handed. Whether we like it or not, we are being forced to play a game, and we are losing. The attack against Mrs Hopkins, an adorable lady who is loved by all, was designed to rouse a reaction. It was intended to make us angry, and it worked. The attack against Jack Fuller was made with the intention of making us feel vulnerable. The Postman wanted to show us that we can't control even the simplest aspects of our lives, like our food. He was letting us know he could make us eat terrible things if he wanted.'

Murmurs rose up from the crowd and Ian was happy that Jack had stayed at home to catch up on some sleep.

'Thankfully, it was not the case,' the mayor quickly added, trying to avoid further panic. 'But the fact remains, by filling our hearts with anger and a feeling of vulnerability, he has made us easy victims of his manipulation, and this is why he was able to push one of us to commit murder. He doesn't need to perform physical violence because he knows that we can be manipulated into doing it for him. Brett Greyson's death was a great victory for him and a terrible defeat for us. Worst of all, I'm afraid that it will not be his last victory. But that's up to us.'

The mayor studied the faces of his audience. Faces that stared back at him, ghostly white and deeply troubled.

'I'm not a psychologist, but it seems clear to me. This maniac, whoever he is, needs to feel powerful, needs to play God, and he has chosen Mirebury as his playground. We're trying to catch him, and I hope we do, but if we're going to survive this game, we need to stop playing into his hands. Don't let our town be torn apart! Don't let him make us hate and fear each other! That's what he wants!'

Everybody jumped to their feet and cheered loudly. Their faces were still troubled but the mayor's speech had stirred them.

Ian smiled as he clapped his hands. It was an important step towards fighting back, even if he knew the game was far from won. He'd heard many speeches before and knew that their effect was generally short-lived. Mirebury needed to take more practical action, and he had an idea.

'I'm going to ask the mayor if I can share my idea,' Ian whispered to Charlotte.

'Yes. It might just work.'

He remained standing as everybody else sat again.

The mayor noticed him and understood the prompt.

'Ian, you'd like to propose a plan of action?'

'That's right, Mayor Larkins.'

'I would like you all to listen to him carefully. Once he has explained his idea, I think that we should vote for or against. Come on up, Ian.'

'Thank you.'

He took his place at the microphone, looked out across the assembly, and cleared his throat.

'As the mayor explained, I've been involved, along with several other residents, in carrying out nightly rounds of Mirebury.'

'It hasn't worked too bloody well!' somebody commented.

'Yes,' Ian admitted, unsuccessfully attempting to locate where the voice had come from. 'That is true, and that's why I think we need to try another line of attack. The worst way to handle this situation is to do nothing. I think we need an innovative approach. We need to disrupt the Postman's *modus operandi*.'

'His what now?' another voice yelled.

Laughter and murmurs filled the room for an instant.

'His method.' Ian went on quickly. 'The way he plays his game. His victims seem to be randomly selected, so there is no way of knowing who he'll try to provoke next. But what his attack on Mitchell Somers has shown is that the result of his attacks can be tragic. Perhaps somebody here tonight will be his next target.'

Ian made a sweeping gesture and everybody looked at each other. His aim wasn't to make them more anxious than they already were, but to make them aware of the need to act swiftly and decisively.

'Who can say how he or she will react if the Postman provokes them next; striking at the heart, pulling the right strings, just as he did with Mr Somers?'

A cold wave washed across the assembly as each person imagined receiving a nasty surprise capable of sending them over the edge.

'I believe my idea will either be a stunning failure or provide us with an absolute victory. If you agree to give it a try, it will require the complete cooperation of every household.'

Ian paused.

They were listening, eager to know what he had to propose.

He hoped it wouldn't be a grave mistake, that it wouldn't push the Postman to take his deadly game to another level.

23

That evening, while most of the other townsfolk were at the meeting, one woman stayed at home and watched television distractedly. Now and then, she would get up to stoke the fire and look outside, wondering if anybody would come to visit her. She was hoping her sisters would call on her.

As she peered between the curtains for the umpteenth time, she saw a shadow flicker like a black flame near her letterbox. She understood instantly. The Postman had just made a delivery.

She knew she was supposed to call Sergeant Manning, and that she shouldn't leave the safety of her house, but she wasn't afraid. She found herself walking to the door and opening it, letting the protecting warmth escape her home. Her feet carried her to the letterbox.

The envelope had no stamp, and her name was printed in capital letters. It set alarm bells ringing, but it also made her curiosity grow. As she stared at the envelope, hypnotised by her own name, she simply couldn't help herself.

She raised her eyes and looked back at the house, where she could see smoke billowing from the chimney. If her husband had been there, he might have taken the letter and cast it into the fire, or he might have opened it himself and reflected coolly on how to proceed. But he wasn't there to tell her what to do and impose his logic.

She looked up and down her street. She seemed to be alone, yet there was no shaking the feeling that hidden eyes were watching, waiting for her to make her decision.

The envelope felt heavier than it was. A burden in her hand. It was begging to be opened. She wondered whether she'd been drugged, because her senses weren't sharp. She felt numb. Was it possible for an envelope to be laced with some kind of poison that could seep into the skin and take immediate effect? The idea was surely ridiculous, wasn't it?

She turned the envelope over, then glanced up and down the length of the street again, trying to locate the shadow from which she imagined the Postman was watching her. She knew she didn't have the willpower to resist and figured that he, too, must have known. So she slid a glossy fingernail under one end of the flap and tore the envelope open.

Her nervous fingers fumbled with the letter, pulling it out and unfolding it. She was thrilled, bizarrely, almost incomprehensibly. But she knew why, in fact. She'd been chosen. In a way, it was an honour. The Postman had decided to play with her.

The message was short and printed neatly like her name on the envelope. Her relief was instantaneous. It wasn't a threat, or bad news, or even a provocation. She was being made a proposition.

She folded the letter again and looked at it, shaking in her hands. She wasn't sure why she was shaking. It wasn't out of fear—not entirely anyway, because what troubled her mind was more apprehension than fear. A knot of disgust and guilt formed in her stomach as she realised what it was. The proposition, which was grotesque and beyond justification by any stretch of the imagination, enticed her, tempted her so deliciously in a way she'd never been tempted before in her safe and honest life.

She looked at her house, her nice warm house where she ought to be sitting back in her armchair, finding comfort in the crackling fire.

Then she turned back to the street, pushed the letter deep into her coat pocket, and walked away into the dark. She would accept to meet the Postman, despite the nagging sense of danger telling her to go back home. She wanted to hear more about this proposition.

Her feet took her along the road and beyond the limits of Mirebury, into the moorland.

She waited at the designated spot, Foxglove Hollow, for what seemed an eternity. All the locals knew the hollow, but they rarely visited it, with the exception of hikers and loners. It was one of those places everybody explores as a teenager and then, the rite of passage out of way, forgets about. There were theories of all kinds about how it had got its name, but nobody had ever seen foxglove growing there, making the hollow all the more enigmatic. It was the best place on the moors for a secret meeting, being lower than the surrounding land and hidden from view. Shaped like a triangular scar, it rose steeply on two sides and was deepest and more treacherous where those two sides met. At the other end, the land rose more gently, and a narrow gap between crags allowed access. As long as one remained on hard ground, standing on the rocks, there was no danger. But if the earth began to move underfoot or felt spongy, it was time to hurry back to the nearest solid patch. If you broke through the surface and sank into the slime, getting out again unaided was no mean feat, and John Phelps would be robbed of a chance to dig a grave.

With this in mind, even though she knew exactly where she was, she couldn't help but feel completely lost out there in the wild. She was putting herself at the Postman's mercy. He could do as he pleased with her. But she remained there, staring up at the tors standing like sentinels above the hollow, waiting for him to come to her.

As far as she knew, she would be the only inhabitant of Mirebury to speak to him. The idea was as exhilarating as it was frightening.

The minutes dragged along slowly, as though time itself was caught in a quagmire, and the longer she waited, the more she wanted to leave that horrid place as quickly as possible.

She wouldn't be able to stay out on the moor all night. Perhaps somebody would come looking for her and demand an explanation for her uncharacteristic behaviour. Perhaps somebody would see her and suspect her of having an affair. That begged the question, didn't it? Perhaps that was precisely what she was doing.

The urge to leave the hollow and run back to town was beginning to override her desire to hear more about the

Postman's proposition when a shape as black as pitch appeared. It approached rapidly, looked down to check that she was alone, then weaved its way down between the crags.

Regret wracked her as the figure drew close, its face hidden by a hood. If he decided to kill her, she would be helpless. She had never felt so at risk in all her life.

'Thank you for coming,' he said, as though they were at a business lunch in a chic London restaurant, except that his voice was muffled and flat.

'Don't mention it. Your letter interested me.' She could hardly believe how calm she sounded.

'I thought it would. I've been watching you.'

He noticed her shudder.

'Don't worry. Not just you. I've been watching everybody in town. I know what you want, and I'm more than happy to help you obtain it.'

She couldn't see his face at all, his lips were hidden in darkness, but she was sure he smiled.

'Will you do as instructed?'

'Yes, I will.'

'Excellent. It's only a small act on your behalf, but I'm sure you'll agree your reward will be immensely satisfying.'

'How do you know your plan will turn out the way you expect it to?'

'I don't *know* that it will, but it will.' His words were so reassuring, his intentionally flat tone so confident.

She dared ask him the ultimate question.

'Where is my...'

'No, no, no! Questions weren't part of the deal.'

'Sorry.'

'Do as I instruct and everything will go to plan. Everything you desire will be yours.'

He was so persuasive that she dared not doubt his words a moment longer.

'I'll do it.'

Then he was gone. He hurried back out of the hollow and

133

vanished behind a towering crag, leaving her stunned by how short and to the point the meeting had been. She almost wondered whether it had taken place at all.

24

Ian's plan was implemented the next day. Its simplicity was what guaranteed it gain general support. The consensus was that it was worth a shot. George did his round as usual, only this time, he didn't deliver any mail. Instead, he covered every letterbox with a plastic bag and every mail slot with a plastic sheet and firmly sealed them off with duct tape. He then attached a printed note informing the household that it would be necessary to collect one's mail in person from the post office until further notice. George would remain at the post office and send an SMS or email to let residents know if they had any mail. The note also stressed that under no circumstances was the cover to be removed.

It was a slow and tedious task, but George was confident the idea would prove helpful.

'Time will tell,' Mrs Hopkins told him that evening, catching him on the way home. 'Such a drastic measure can only stay in place on a temporary basis and it's going to cause quite a bit of inconvenience for some of us, but it's worth a try.'

'I'm sure George will allow me to collect your mail for you if you'd like.'

'That's lovely of you, Ian.'

'It's the least I can do. It was my idea after all.'

'You're handling this whole odious business admirably,' she said, leaning closer to emphasise her words. 'That's more than I can say for a lot of the townsfolk. I don't like what's happening to them. Some days, I don't even want to step out the front door.'

'But you must, you know. You mustn't stay locked away.'

'I'll be just fine, Ian. Don't worry about this old bird. She's flown through many a storm in her time.'

'I don't doubt it.'

'Who's keeping watch tonight?'

'It's my turn.'

A dark look passed across her face.

'You watch your back, my lad. Don't go playing the hero. That new lady librarian's going to need you in one piece.' She shot him a cheeky wink.

'I may as well stay inside tonight and not bother about going on patrol. Nothing seems to get past our Mrs Hopkins.'

A few minutes before nine o'clock, Ian dressed himself in warm, dark clothes and armed himself with his cricket bat, a torch, and a camera. He turned every light in his house off and peered out from behind the curtains of his bedroom window. The street was as still as an oil painting.

He'd decided his primary duty would be to carefully inspect every household's letterbox to ensure that none of the plastic covering had been removed or tampered with in any way. A missing or damaged cover would act as a warning bell, alerting him to the likelihood that mischief had taken place.

A gentle but chill breeze swept along his street. Its bite would help him stay awake and on the ball. Rustling leaves played an almost inaudible concert and the stars in the clear sky observed the mortal world below. Mirebury almost gave the impression of being at ease, sleeping comfortably, blanketed in a tranquil night.

After checking that the cover was still attached to his old, scratched letterbox, he crossed the street. He could sense the unease that pervaded behind the locked doors and barred windows of his elderly neighbour's house. She was putting on a brave face, but the Postman's first victim would never fully recover from the horror that had been inflicted upon her.

He continued along the street, heading through the darkness towards the centre of town, checking every letterbox and mail slot as he walked. Occasionally, he would detect a subtle movement as a curtain moved, almost imperceptibly. People were keeping watch, wondering who was out there. He imagined them being startled at the sight of a shadow armed with a cricket bat, haunting the street, before recognising the inoffensive school teacher and remembering that tonight was his round.

It reassured him that they were watching. If he encountered the Postman, it wouldn't go unnoticed. They would rush out of their homes and come to his aid, overpowering their tormentor with the force of their numbers.

A curtain snapped shut as Ian passed one of the houses. The fear was palpable.

At least, he hoped that's what would happen. Would they really come to his rescue if it came to the crunch? Or would they simply watch him being slaughtered as they cowered in terror behind their bedroom windows. The more he thought about it, the less certain he felt, so he tried to stop thinking about it at all, and took comfort in the knowledge that the Postman hadn't actually attacked anybody with his own two hands.

He continued his patrol until he'd walked every street in town and checked almost every letterbox. His feet were sore and his eyelids were growing heavy. As he passed the church shortly after two o'clock, he saw that candlelight was flickering behind the stained-glass windows of the sacristy. At the start of his patrol, there had been no light at all inside the church.

He climbed over the stone wall of the churchyard and walked carefully up to the window. He was alone and vulnerable, now exposed by a kaleidoscope of light, and a shiver scurried down his spine as though traced by an icy finger. He spun around, but nothing stirred.

He turned back, feeling foolish, and was now glad there was nobody around to see him. He approached the window and peered through it, pushing aside the fear that he would behold a sight more horrifying than his mind was capable of withstanding.

He released a sigh of relief. Father Godfrey was kneeling before a congregation of candles, so deep in prayer he failed to notice the figure observing him as though he were an animal in a zoo. Despite the cold, his head was crowned with beads of sweat and his face was distorted.

He backed away from the window and turned around, and for a split second, he was sure he saw a tiny red light gleaming like a demon's eye among the crumbling headstones of the old graveyard.

The instant was so brief that Ian told himself he was letting his imagination run wild, but the pit in his stomach was real, as were the goose bumps that rose on his skin. He gripped his bat with both hands and stepped through the obscurity that clung to his feet like thick mud. The tiny red point of light had been ephemeral, but he homed in on where it had been as though he could still see it.

Once he thought he'd arrived at the headstone where the light had been, he knew he had to switch his torch on. But that required lowering his bat and exposing himself to danger.

He looked around, but it was too dark to see. He shivered. He had no choice. He needed to use his torch. Lowering his bat, he removed the torch from his coat and switched it on.

No sooner had he pointed it towards the ground at his feet than he saw what had caused the demon's eye. He hadn't been imagining it after all. It was a half-smoked cigarette, and it was still smouldering.

He knelt down, stubbed the cigarette out, and studied it closely. There was writing printed around it, just above the filter—*Marlboro.*

He dropped it into a pocket and got out of the churchyard as quickly as possible. Out on the street, he tried to pull himself together, but his nerves were failing.

He glanced back at the stained-glass window. While Father Godfrey was praying in the church, a demon was playing in the churchyard.

25

As the funeral procession crawled towards the church, Father Godfrey pulled back the sleeve of his cassock and looked at his watch. They were right on time, but the cortège was short and the churchyard was far from crowded. He'd been hoping the entire town would gather to bid farewell to an honest man and to ponder the tragedy of his violent end, but many residents had decided to stay away from the church, either out of hatred for Brett or fear that violence would consume the gathering and more blood would be shed.

Laura Greyson and her daughter, Becky, were in the car behind the hearse, which was driven by Mayor Larkins. They too would be disappointed.

Ian, Charlotte, Mary, and Jack and his family were gathered together beside the old well in the churchyard, watching in silence as the hearse drew to a stop by the lychgate. Harry Newcombe was further back, leaning against the side of the church and staring absently at the clouds of pungent cigarette smoke he was blowing.

'You were wrong after all, Jack,' Ian mused.

'About what?'

'You thought that Brett's wouldn't be the only funeral this weekend.'

'Father Godfrey was wrong,' he corrected his friend. 'He'd been expecting more violence. I was just repeating what he'd told me.'

The bell tolled.

'What's this talk of more violence?' Mrs Hopkins interrupted them, her voice fragile with concern.

'Evil begets evil,' Charlotte explained, as the mayor opened the door of his car for Laura Greyson.

The pallbearers removed Brett's coffin from the hearse and proceeded through the lychgate and past the small gathering.

Father Godfrey was waiting by the church entrance, his face tired from lack of sleep and too many hours spent on his knees, engrossed in desperate prayer.

'Where is everybody?' Jack asked, looking around.

'They're all at home,' Ian replied quietly. 'Their doors are bolted shut, and they're trying to work out which of their neighbours is the Postman, and which of them suspect *them* of being the Postman.'

'If I were the Postman, I'd be here. That would be the smart thing to do. I'd be right here, right now,' Jack remarked.

'As logical as they may be, it's best not to make statements like that too loudly.'

'Is somebody with Jenny and Alison Somers?' Emily Fuller asked.

'Doctor Sykes told me Jenny's sisters have come to town.'

'They aren't coming to church?'

'No, I don't think so.'

'I can't blame them,' Charlotte added, whispering as the coffin passed. 'It'd be just too difficult.'

Laura and Becky Greyson followed the pallbearers into the church, disappearing into the stone sanctuary like a pair of phantoms. Apart from exchanging a few words with Father Godfrey, they hadn't spoken to anybody.

Even now, they couldn't really understand what had happened. They hadn't seen the provocative photograph and they hadn't spoken to the Somers family since the murder, but they both accepted Alison's assurance that the photo must have been a fake and that her friend's father had never touched her.

Father Godfrey indicated for those present to follow him into the church.

The bell continued to toll for Brett Greyson, ringing out across Mirebury, and Ian wondered if Mitchell Somers could hear that sacred sound, wherever he may be. He also wondered whether the Postman was listening, wherever *he* may be.

The mourners took their places along the pews and many began to pray the moment they were seated.

Father Godfrey stood at the pulpit and surveyed his diminishing flock solemnly.

'Dearly beloved, we are gathered here today to bid farewell to Brett Greyson. He was a loving husband, father, friend, and respected neighbour. His tragic and unexpected passing from this world to the next has pierced the very soul of our town, adding grief to the turmoil that has of late been testing our faith and courage. We are not here today to torment ourselves over the circumstances of Brett's passing. Nor are we here to fall prey to the manipulative hand of the great deceiver. We are here to remember the life of a man who held a special place in our hearts. He was a father who protected his family, and a neighbour who always sought to help his fellow man.

'Brett is with the Lord now, but we are still here, living side by side in the town he loved. He would want us to be strong, to carry on, and to fight to prevent our town from falling into disarray, for he was a down-to-earth, no-nonsense man.'

Muffled sobbing could be heard throughout the otherwise silent congregation.

'A society in disorder, stained by distrust and internal strife, is an easy victim for the great deceiver, for he who would have our hearts filled with anger, hatred, and suspicion. It's not fashionable to talk about evil nowadays. Misguided. Deranged. Troubled. These words are considered more sophisticated, more nuanced. But whatever you choose to call it, evil exists. It's out there, and we need to be on guard, lest it enters into us.'

Ian looked around. Everybody was listening to Father Godfrey's words, sitting stone-faced or wiping their eyes dry, but he asked himself whether they were really *hearing* what he was telling them. These were wise words of counsel. The Postman was playing a morbid game, some kind of twisted sociological study, and so far, Mirebury was playing into his hands.

Father Godfrey instructed the congregation to sing a hymn before hurriedly descending from the pulpit and approaching a

141

figure who was waiting in the shadows beside the organ.

Jack nudged Ian with his elbow. 'Look,' he whispered against the chorus. 'Sergeant Manning's over there, and he's sharing some news with Father Godfrey.'

'You think that...'

'Another death,' Jack cut in.

Ian shook his head.

'Why won't people understand what's happening? We're doing exactly what he wants!'

As the hymn came to its end, Father Godfrey regained his place at the pulpit and the sergeant left the church.

'Harry Newcombe will now read us a passage,' he continued, doing his best to sound calm and reassuring.

The publican made his way up to the pulpit, looking nervous.

'Thank you, father, but before I read the passage, and I pray you will excuse my deviation from procedure, I think we would all like very much to know what news Sergeant Manning has just shared with you.'

Father Godfrey smiled uncomfortably and raised his hands peremptorily to calm the fold.

'Harry, I really don't think this is the appropriate time.'

A cry of protest rang out and filled the church with anxious echoes.

'Tell us, father!'

'Have they found Mitchell?'

'Hang him, the murderer!'

'No, vengeance is mine...'

'It's not vengeance we want; it's justice!'

'String him up, I say!'

Laura and Becky Greyson, who had been weeping quietly, were now bawling bitterly.

'Quiet!' Father Godfrey boomed.

Silence reigned once more.

'You are in the house of God!' he reminded them with a voice that was stern and commanding, a contrast to his usually soothing tone.

'I will tell you what Sergeant Manning told me, but I want you all to leave the church immediately afterwards so that I may be alone with the departed's close family.'

Every head nodded silently.

'Sergeant Manning has just informed me that the person who has been tormenting us has been found dead.'

The congregation was stunned for an instant. Then the victory cries began.

'Hallelujah!'

'Glory be!'

'It's the Lord's will!'

'We are delivered from the claws of Satan!'

Some people sprang from their pews and rushed for the door while others remained seated or took their time finding their feet, as though not quite convinced they were really awake.

'Is he really dead?' Charlotte asked herself, as Mrs Hopkins began to pray aloud, showing no intention of leaving the church.

Ian turned to Jack to read his friend's thoughts on his face. But it was Jack's mouth that communicated his opinion, and the word it uttered wasn't one of praise or thanksgiving.

'Bullshit!'

26

Art Rekeby was behind all this, Sergeant Manning thought to himself, still shaking his head. He hadn't expected this outcome at all and couldn't help but feel that he'd failed Mirebury. This had been his big chance to prove himself to the townsfolk, to show them he wasn't just a backwater bobby who was only good for finding lost cats and giving defensive driving talks, and he'd failed. He'd caught Art getting up to mischief several times, mostly after a few too many drinks, but he would never in a million years have suspected the young man of being twisted enough to carry out such a destructive campaign of terror.

The detective in command of the investigation had called in a forensics squad while Sergeant Manning had cordoned off the street. They were in the process of bagging whatever they could find; hair, dirt, crumbs, any clues that might lead them to Art's murderer.

It seemed obvious that the murderer had been a man, and a strong one at that. In fact, there had probably been several men. Sergeant Manning couldn't imagine an individual being physically capable of doing *that*.

A police photographer finished taking snapshots of the victim's body from every angle and distance. Art had been nailed to his bedroom wall with a pitchfork through the neck. His feet dangled an inch or so above a pool of blood. His bed was covered in photographs, intimate and pornographic shots of Cherry Somers. The images followed much the same theme as the photo in which the girl had been featured with Brett Greyson, but according to the police photographer, these shots, unlike the one that had triggered Mitchell Somers's frenzied attack on Brett Greyson, had not been digitally edited. They ranged from glamour to explicit. In the softest, she could be seen hiding her nipples with cherries and smiling enticingly at the camera. Another showed her having a bubble bath. In one of the more shocking close-ups, her mouth was wide open and her tongue bejewelled with pearly white drops, and in the most daring of all, she was squatting naked on top of Mirebury's decommissioned red telephone box, using a well-placed finger to direct a stream of urine arching down onto a parked motorbike.

Sergeant Manning asked himself whether Mitchell had somehow found out about these pictures, maybe from his daughter, and come out of hiding to set the record straight. It was a nightmare scenario, his duty as a police officer forcing him to suspect one of the men who meant the most to him in the whole world.

Was it possible that his first taste of murder had given him a thirst for blood? The sergeant had never known Mitchell to be a violent man, but recent events had brought previously unquestioned assumptions into the spotlight. It was now common knowledge that Mitchell was capable of losing his temper in a big way. CID described him as *possibly armed and dangerous* and warned the public *not to approach him* but to *contact police immediately* if they spotted him. It was out of the sergeant's hands now that the big boys were in town, but that wouldn't stop him from trying to figure out what had gone on. Assuming Mitchell was indeed involved in Art's murder, who could have helped him? Who could his accomplice or accomplices have been, and where were they now? In any case, if he'd come out of hiding for the occasion, he'd since disappeared again. Part of Sergeant Manning wanted to find his friend, but another part wanted him to remain free.

The CID inspector interrupted Sergeant Manning's train of thought.

'How are you holding up, sergeant?'

'I still can't believe all this has really happened.'

'Not the usual work of Mirebury's law enforcer, is it?' He patted Sergeant Manning on the back.

They both looked at Art, pinned to the wall like a gruesome

exhibit.

'This is the work of at least two murderers, but more likely three.'

'I agree, sir,' the sergeant added. 'Two to hold him against the wall while the third, perhaps after explaining why he had to die, thrust the fork through his neck.'

The inspector nodded, clearly impressed.

The four prongs of the pitchfork were firmly planted into the wall, far enough to support Art's weight. The feat would have required considerable strength; perhaps even more than Mitchell Somers had in him.

'So, this fellow fits in with the profile of your Postman?'

'Yes, sir. These photographs were probably used to produce the fake one, as an analysis of his computer will hopefully prove.'

'What else?'

'The bicycle out back fits the description I've heard of the Postman's, especially the peculiar grating sound it makes, and you can bet London to a brick the soil in the old wheelbarrow will match the soil at the cemetery. Likewise, the tools found under his bed are likely to be those used to desecrate Mr Hopkins's grave.'

'We'll see if forensics can confirm your suspicions, sergeant. That sounds like a solid enough case. I'm afraid catching his murderers won't be so easy a mystery to solve though. They were surprisingly thorough in their efforts to deny us any evidence.'

Sergeant Manning nodded silently, but he wasn't too concerned about that. Art had got what he deserved. Catching the Postman's killers wasn't a priority for him. On the other hand, he was curious to know who had solved the puzzle.

27

The town's reaction to the news of the Postman's murder was mostly one of great relief. The truth of the matter was that Art Rekeby was a young man who had never been appreciated by the majority of the townsfolk. It was widely understood that he'd taken advantage of Cherry Somers's unbridled sexual urges and introduced her to some bizarre carnal pleasures, the practice of which even women twice her age were completely unaware. He had always been a bit of a loner too, and was described by many as a *shady chap* or a *strange sort*. Frankly speaking, the announcement of his brutal death was not met with the shedding of many tears. Mirebury was rather relieved that the Postman was Art.

But not everybody was so easily convinced. Ian almost regretted having come up with the idea of putting the town's letterboxes out of service and wanted to put an end to the measure in the hope that the real Postman would continue his attacks. Jack, Jonathan, and Charlotte were among those who shared Ian's stubborn refusal to accept Art Rekeby as the culprit. He invited them all to his house that evening.

'Thanks for coming, everyone. Make yourselves at home while I fetch us a few drinks. Gin? Scotch? Beer?'

They weren't there for a social visit, but he figured they may as well try to make the atmosphere as pleasant as possible. He emptied some crisps into one bowl and peanuts into another, then poured their drinks.

They raised their glasses.

'To our dear home Mirebury, that she may see us through these dark days,' Jack toasted.

'To Mirebury.'

'Let's cut to the chase,' Jonathan suggested. 'We all seem to agree that the notion that Art Rekeby was behind all of this is ludicrous.'

'Absolutely,' Charlotte agreed. 'I barely knew the lad, but even on the rare occasions we crossed paths, I could tell he wasn't clever enough or twisted enough to pull off a campaign of terror like this. Sure, he seemed a little creepy, and wouldn't stop leering at me, but he didn't deserve to die for that.'

Jack spoke his mind next.

'I think everybody has accepted his guilt so easily for two reasons. Firstly, he's always been the target of a lot of animosity. Parents despise him because they're afraid he'll corrupt their daughters and be a bad influence on their sons. Most of the young women in town hate him because he's a sexual deviant and gets up to all kinds of perverse antics with Cherry, and a number of young men are green with envy. The second reason is that they so desperately want an end to this torment. Art's the perfect scapegoat, and the Postman was well aware of that. The crime scene was packed full of evidence against him and that was enough to convince them he was the one. What do you think, Ian?'

'I agree, Jack. It's precisely *because* of all the evidence against him that I think he's innocent. The whole thing stinks of a set-up.'

'Yes, but who would have set him up?' Jonathan asked.

They looked at each other.

'The Postman, I suppose,' Jack said.

'Do you suspect somebody else, Jonathan?' Ian asked.

He shook his head. 'No, I don't really. I just want to keep my mind open.'

'The Postman must have gained access to Art's house and framed him,' Ian suggested. 'He planted his own bicycle and tools there. He clearly knew, somehow, about Art's tendency to take photographs of his kinky antics with Cherry Somers, just like he seems to know so much about everybody in Mirebury.'

'That makes sense,' Charlotte agreed. 'The Postman killed him and then planted evidence against him.'

'Probably not,' Ian replied with an enigmatic look on his face.

'What are you hiding, Ian? Do we have any other details about the crime scene?' Jonathan asked somewhat sharply.

Ian sipped pensively at his beer before replying.

'Stop teasing us, Ian,' Charlotte pleaded.

'Spit it out!' Jack ordered him.

'Calm down,' he told them. 'I spoke to Simon briefly today. He's been very busy, of course, and he's still trying to come to terms with Brett's death. But we had a quick chat. He told me the crime unit ordered him to keep quiet about the case, but he let slip a little.'

'Did he indeed?' Charlotte asked, leaning closer.

'He said they were searching for clues to the *identities* of the *killers*.'

Charlotte gasped, and Jack almost sprayed a mouthful of beer. Jonathan frowned, his mind racing.

'He was murdered by more than one person?' Jonathan asked.

'So it would seem.'

'That means the real Postman didn't kill him,' Jack said.

'He must have manipulated one of us,' Charlotte said. 'That's what he does.'

'More than one of us,' Ian reminded her.

'He always uses a letterbox to wreak havoc,' Jonathan observed.

'So you think somebody in town received a tip-off of some kind?' Jack asked.

'I guess so,' Jonathan said. 'That's probably what happened.'

'No. That doesn't make sense,' Ian interrupted.

'Why not?' Jack looked puzzled.

'Think about it,' Ian continued. 'Somebody received a message from the Postman indicating that somebody else in town is the Postman.' He rubbed his face in confusion.

'I see what you mean,' Charlotte agreed. 'It doesn't make sense.'

They sat without speaking for a minute as they drank and deliberated. Ian was starting to think the Postman would never be caught.

'Is there a way we can think of that he could lead somebody to believe Art was the Postman without making it seem he'd left a message indicating that?'

Nobody replied. It was an excellent question, but one that was practically impossible to answer without being as cunning and imaginative as the Postman himself. Perhaps he would be content to let everybody believe Art had been behind it all. Ian wondered whether that was the best outcome they could hope for. The Postman might just disappear, leaving the mystery unexplained; a perpetual shadow over Mirebury.

'What about...' Charlotte began, but then hesitated.

'Go ahead, Charlotte,' Ian encouraged her. 'We need ideas. Give us whatever you've got.'

'Well, it sounds simplistic,' she went on, hesitating.

'Simple explanations are often the most realistic,' Jonathan suggested.

'I was just wondering whether maybe the Postman left a message for somebody that hinted discreetly that Art was the Postman. A letter supposedly from somebody who saw Art doing something strange or suspicious but was too scared to identify him or herself.'

They thought about it.

'Very well,' Jonathan said. 'But if that were the case, the letter would have been addressed to a person who could act accordingly; that is, Sergeant Manning. But I can't imagine for a minute that our sergeant is capable of killing a man in cold blood.'

'That's a good point,' Charlotte conceded. 'But if anybody else had received such a letter, they would have gone straight to the police.'

'Are we sure about that?' Ian asked the others.

Jonathan's eyebrows arched, and Jack and Charlotte just gave him a blank stare.

'Correct me if I'm wrong, Ian, but you're suggesting somebody received a letter of the kind Charlotte described, believed it, and decided to take the law into their own hands,' Jonathan said. 'He or she told another person, or other people, and they lynched Art. Is that what you're saying?'

'I don't want to believe it any more than you, but we have to consider the possibility.'

A low whistle escaped Jonathan's lips.

'Where does this leave us?' Jack asked, trying to make sense of all the speculation.

'Back where we started,' Ian replied, looking defeated.

'You're right, Ian. We're back where we started, so let's work with that,' Jonathan said. 'Let's start again. We need to stop the Postman. That's our objective. We have to catch this psychopath and put an end to all this chaos. Do we believe the Postman is a local or are we still convinced he must be an outsider?'

They looked at each but sipped their drinks instead of replying.

Charlotte spoke first. 'He has to be a local. He knows the people of Mirebury and how to manipulate them. I think it's safe to say he knows you better than I do, or even Ian. He's not an outsider, or a newcomer. The strings being pulled aren't obvious ones. At a puppet show, you have to be close to see them. Don't you agree? I think this is the same. It may be less so for the attack on Jack, but it's definitely the case for the deliveries made to Mrs Hopkins and Mitchell Somers, and the plot against Art. Only a local could have seen which strings to pull.'

Jack grunted his agreement and Jonathan hummed.

'I completely agree,' Ian said. 'We also know it's a man.'

'We do?' Charlotte asked.

'It has to be,' Jack replied. 'There's no way a woman could have dug up Clive Hopkins's skull.'

'Are you sure?' Charlotte asked. 'Not all women are weaker than men.'

'Of course,' Jack hastened to reply. 'But can you think of a woman in Mirebury who'd be capable of it?'

'I guess not,' she admitted. 'In any case, violent psychopaths are generally men.'

'Both good points,' Jonathan said. 'We need to narrow down

the list. This is all we've got so far. Do we agree? The Postman is a man from Mirebury who's fit and strong. Who do we have?'

They remained silent for a minute, parading suspects through their minds.

'Sergeant Manning fits the bill,' Ian offered, not sounding at all convinced.

'Are you serious?' Jack asked.

'I don't suspect him for an instant, Jack. But we have to do this thoroughly.'

'I guess you're right. All the same, it can't be our Simon. I'm telling you it's not possible. It doesn't make sense. Brett Greyson was a good friend of his. They've been mates since childhood and never had a falling out as far I know. His grief is real. Mitchell Somers is also a friend of his. It can't be him. It just can't be. Not Simon.'

'Doctor Sykes,' Charlotte suggested, eager to know how they would react.

'Gordon?' Jonathan asked incredulously. 'You're joking?'

'We can't rule him out, can we?'

'I guess not,' Jonathan admitted, looking from Ian to Jack.

'Who else?' Jack asked. 'Who has a grudge?'

'Damian Granger,' Ian said. 'I find him quite likeable, but we can't rule him out. He may not be all that young, but he's a tough one, and we know he's not too fond of people in general. He has a grudge against everybody, unless they buy his mushrooms and bootleg brandy.'

The others frowned, but nobody replied.

'We have George and Harry,' Jonathan said without any great conviction.

The others considered those names.

'Aiden and Gavin,' he continued.

It seemed futile.

'John and Edward,' Ian added.

'John Phelps?' Jonathan asked.

Ian shrugged.

'He's strong for his age, and he knows all about digging

graves,' Charlotte pointed out.

'That's true,' Jonathan admitted. 'But you and Ian don't know him like Jack and I do. While I don't doubt he has a skeleton or two in his closet, he has the greatest and most genuine esteem for Mary and her late husband. John was at his funeral, of course, and he was a broken man that day.'

'I couldn't agree more,' Jack said. 'Who else did we say? Edward—the mayor? No. He loves Mirebury more than anybody. That's why we keep re-electing him almost unanimously. And what about the speech he gave? That came from the heart. Not a chance.'

'What about Father Godfrey?' Charlotte said. 'He's probably stronger than he looks.'

The men stared at her wide-eyed.

'What? You're not so naive as to think men of the cloth are all angels, are you?'

They looked at each other.

'Not Father Godfrey either. I've known him my whole life,' Jonathan said, shaking his head. 'So have you, Jack. It's not just a matter of being a priest. He's a truly righteous man and loves Mary like a sister. In fact, he considers us all his brothers and sisters, and sons and daughters.'

'Absolutely,' Jack agreed. 'I'm not one of his sheep by any means, but it can't be him. He's a fine man.'

'It's not even worth talking about motivation,' Jonathan mused. 'We have a psychopath on our hands. I don't think we could even begin to fathom what could drive him. We have no reason to suspect any of these men of being criminally insane.'

'They've all had their ups and downs,' Jack said. 'Perhaps we all have at one point or another. Who can ever really know what's going on inside anyone else's head?'

'Damian, Gavin, and Aiden have been through their fair share of rough patches,' Jonathan pointed out.

'They have?' Ian asked.

Jack and Jonathan exchanged a glance, the kind that indicated it was a long story.

153

'Tell us,' Charlotte said.

'I'll give you the short version,' Jonathan said. 'As you know, Ian, Art's parents were killed in a car accident. It was years ago now, in the early hours of the morning, around this time of the year. It was as foggy as could be, with probably next to no visibility on the road through the moors. The collision was head-on and at high speed.'

Ian and Charlotte were listening intently. Jack was shaking his head slowly.

'Nobody found out about it until later that day. Art had been staying with his grandmother, a dear old soul, while his parents had been off partying. It was Aiden's mother in the other car. She'd survived the crash, passed out most likely, and stumbled into town when she came to. All three of them had been blind drunk. Aiden's mother, Tara, had been on Damian's demon juice. She couldn't remember any of what had happened, except that she'd been drinking with Damian and Paul Kemble, Gavin's dad. Back in those days, Paul used to spend a lot of time with Damian in his caravan. They were like brothers.'

'She'd been alone in the car?' Charlotte asked.

'That's the question. She was no longer with Aiden's dad in those days. He'd run off on her, and she swore she'd been alone in the car. But no one knows for sure.'

'Did Art hate Aiden because of the accident?'

'I'm sure he did. They all hate each other. Aiden doesn't care much for his mother. Art despised Damian and blamed him for getting Tara drunk. Damian and Paul fell out over money and women years before Paul died. Ever since, Damian has grown increasingly reclusive, as has Tara. You'll have noticed you don't see either of them hanging around town more than strictly necessary.'

'Did Damian, Gavin, and Aiden hate Art?' Ian asked.

'Maybe they did. They might have resented Art linking them to his parents' death, thinking it was somehow their fault. Gavin and Aiden were also jealous of Art's relationship with Cherry.'

'They weren't the only ones,' Jack said. 'Just about every

154

young man in town was jealous of him. Not to mention some of the older ones.'

Charlotte conveyed her disgust by making a spitting sound.

'Does any of this have a connection to what's happening?' Ian wondered.

'It's hard to say,' Jonathan said. 'It just goes to show there's a lot of history in a small town like Mirebury.'

'You forgot to mention the time Gordon confronted Damian outside The Owl and Moon after John Phelps almost died from eating poisonous mushrooms,' Jack said. 'As well as being an accomplished rugby player, the doctor was quite a boxer in his youth. Smartest move Damian ever made it was, keeping his arse on the barstool and letting the doctor give him an earful. I don't think he's been back to the pub ever since. I don't think he's dared go near John either.'

Ian and Charlotte stared at each other, eyebrows raised.

'Why am I only learning all this just now?' Ian asked.

Jack shrugged.

'I don't know where this gets us,' Jonathan said. 'Most likely, nowhere at all. There's plenty of tension and animosity between just about everyone if you do a little digging. The problem is, we keep coming back to Mary Hopkins. She was the first victim of the Postman, but she's the last person any of us could possibly hold a grudge against.'

'I'm no expert on the topic,' Charlotte said, 'but from what I've read, there doesn't seem to be one single cause of mental imbalance. We know that in many cases, it's the result of unresolved traumatic experiences in childhood, but it can also be triggered by drug abuse, or it can be a congenital condition.'

'It may not be a popular opinion, but some people are just born bad,' Jack said. 'I'm sure of it.'

'I agree,' Charlotte said. 'I've witnessed it first-hand. The world is full of controlling, manipulative people, and they're often very good at hiding who they really are from the rest of us.'

'That's true,' Ian said. 'The Postman is using letterboxes to play with our lives and control us. Is he all that different from an

155

abusive husband or a sexual predator? Or for that matter, from an advertising executive, the head of a multinational corporation, or a stock trader? The games may be different, but the need to win is the same.'

'Do teachers appear on that list?' Charlotte asked, laughing.

Ian wagged his finger at her.

'We provide structure in order to educate and empower,' Jonathan said. 'That's the opposite of manipulation.'

'We can't have everyone in town undergo a psychological assessment,' Jack said.

'No, we can't,' Jonathan agreed. 'It would be legally and logistically impossible.'

'And let's face it, there aren't too many of us who could claim to be perfectly sane,' Jack added. 'It would most likely take years to identity and classify all the different issues present in Mirebury.'

They fought the temptation to laugh.

'In other words, there's no point attempting to determine the motivation or cause,' Charlotte said. 'Is there another angle we're missing?'

'We haven't considered alibis yet,' Ian said.

'We haven't,' Jonathan agreed. 'Is it even worth trying?'

'Isn't it? Do we know who has an alibi for the desecration of Mr Hopkins's grave?' Jack asked.

'It happened at night. Do you have an alibi, Ian?' Jonathan asked.

'I guess not. I was at home, alone in bed.'

'I was in bed with my wife,' Jack said.

'As was I, Jack. Does that constitute an alibi? If a man's wife is a sound sleeper, would she necessarily notice his absence? Even if she does notice, and vouches for her husband, is that really a solid alibi?'

'I see your point,' Ian admitted.

'What about the letters targeting my business?' Jack asked.

'We were having dinner with the Sykes and the Whites,' Ian reminded Jonathan. 'Tim came in with the letter, but it could have been delivered by just about anyone at any time that afternoon or evening.'

'That's right. Being there when Gordon's lad came in with the letter hardly provides an alibi,' Charlotte said.

'It's the same problem for the fake picture of Cherry and Brett,' Jack said. 'The delivery could have been made at any time during the night. Jonathan's right. Establishing solid alibis is next to impossible.'

'That doesn't leave us with much. If only we had a clue,' Charlotte said. 'But the Postman's been so thorough.'

'Now you mention it. There might be one,' Ian told them, remembering what he'd found. It wasn't much, and he'd let it slip his mind, but it was all they had. He looked at them one by one, nodding. 'I almost forgot. I found it the other night while I was on patrol.'

They were speechless.

'Come on then,' Jack broke the silence. 'Spit it out!'

28

The following day was a dark one for Mirebury, both psychologically and meteorologically. Thick fog smothered the town and blocked everything from view. The few inhabitants who had the courage to leave the doubtful security of their own homes moved quickly and silently through the streets like frightened mice. Even though the Postman had been killed, they feared an aftermath, just like a hunter is wary of the final death throes of a dying beast.

None of Mirebury's pupils came to class. Their parents had most likely locked them up in their bedrooms despite the fact that what had happened to Art proved that even a person's most private sanctuary wasn't safe. Jonathan used the student-free day to hold a staff meeting to brainstorm ways to address the emotional and behavioural problems that would inevitably plague the students as a result of the town's descent into chaos.

Jack had one of the quietest days since the discovery of the note claiming he sold human flesh. His usual customers were afraid he too might lose the plot and hack them apart with the meat cleaver he used when he patrolled the town at night. After the deaths of Brett and Art, everybody assumed his friends and neighbours were murderers, and like in the animal kingdom, the strongest inspired the most fear.

While most of Mirebury felt some relief at Art's death, his family and friends—particularly Cherry—were devastated. They refused to believe he was guilty and wouldn't rest until his murderers, stupid enough to be manipulated by the Postman, had been brought to justice.

Art's death had convinced Cherry to leave her bedroom for the first time since the fake photograph had been discovered. Her embarrassment for herself and fear for her father had given way to a hungry anger. Several of her former boyfriends, who were eager to regain her favour, and Art's friends and younger brother, were stalking the foggy streets of Mirebury. The red-haired beauty led the gang like a warrior princess. While the town's other residents hid within their homes or walked quickly along the street, this gang strode proudly and fearlessly. They were armed with tools and weapons of all kinds; picks, hammers, bicycle chains, and fire pokers, and they wouldn't hesitate to use them if necessary. They were seeking any information that would lead them to Art's killers, and nobody dared defy them or refused to answer their questions. They didn't know who to suspect but they were intent upon finding out through the use of harassment and menaces.

Further police reinforcements had been requested and were expected later that day. The contingent already in place was too busy to maintain public order, especially now that another problem requiring their immediate attention had emerged.

Unknown to the furious Cherry, as she stalked the streets, or the empty shell of her mother, locked away inside her house, Mitchell Somers had been found.

29

If his claim was to be believed, Mitchell hadn't meant to kill Brett, just to knock him around. He'd wanted him to beg for forgiveness, and to swear he'd never take advantage of Cherry again—to promise he wouldn't even go near her and would turn right around and go back the way he'd come when he saw her in the street. But instead of apologising, Brett had slain his prize dog. That's what had sent him into a frenzy of rage. When Mitchell left Brett's property with Drover's bloody carcass in his arms, he hadn't realised he was dead.

Later, once he'd come to his senses and buried Drover, he started to ask himself just how hard he'd hit him, and how many times. It wasn't until he checked his phone and listened to the desperate calls from his wife that he knew for certain that Brett's head had been struck one or two blows too many. That's when he had to make the most difficult decision of his life.

It wasn't a Mirebury resident, but a hiker from out of town who had stumbled across Mitchell. He'd been walking in the moors with his dog, in one of the rare wooded areas, when he came across the corpse hanging from the thickest bough of a sturdy tree. The hiker, not recognising the deceased, had checked his pockets, looking for identification, and found his driving licence and a handwritten letter.

The letter detailed the tragic train of events and finished with a heart-breaking final message to his wife and daughter, telling them he was sorry and asking them to forgive him. A life of shame and imprisonment simply wasn't an option for a proud man who loved open spaces and freedom.

He told Cherry he loved her and that none of what had happened was her fault. Brett had abused her. He'd taken advantage of an impressionable adolescent. He said there was no doubt in his mind that she would grow up to be an upstanding woman. He told his wife and daughter to try their very best, every single day, to be happy, and advised them to remain on good terms with the Greysons. They were going to need each other's support and understanding.

'Two murders and a suicide,' the inspector said to himself, placing the letter in an evidence bag.

Sergeant Manning watched helplessly as the crime unit removed the lifeless body of Mitchell Somers from the bough. It was horrible to see him hanging there like a grim offering to the ancient gods of the moors.

Mitchell must have climbed up the tree with the rope in hand, tied it around the bough and his neck, and then jumped. The scene of his death was such a peaceful place, Sergeant Manning couldn't imagine a more beautiful spot in the area to spend one's final moments. He looked away, not wanting the other policemen to see the tears welling in his eyes. He remembered the good times he'd spent with Mitchell, watching the sheep graze while they drank a cup of tea, enjoying a pint of ale at The Owl and Moon, and sometimes leaving town for a trip to the coast to have a dip and eat fish and chips. In his mind, he saw Mitchell, as proud as punch as he received the sheepdog trial award.

How quickly it had all changed.

He remembered seeing Cherry from the top of the church, as a man took her from behind like a dog. He hadn't been able to take his eyes off her. He felt guilty about that now. He shouldn't have looked at his friend's daughter that way, finding pleasure in what he'd witnessed. Mitchell's death only made his guilt and regret stronger.

Sergeant Manning watched as Mitchell was driven away in the coroner's van, the vehicle rolling up and down as it manoeuvred across the gentle contours of the moor and faded into the mounting fog.

'Goodbye, old friend.'

As inexperienced as he was in homicide investigations, it was still clear to the sergeant that the state of Mitchell's body indicated that he'd killed himself some time ago, certainly before Art Rekeby had been murdered. That was the only good news to be had that day. Mitchell was one suspect he was pleased to be able to cross off his list.

30

Charlotte opened Ian's bedroom window just a crack and lit a cigarette. Mirebury's darkest day had given way to a pitch-black night. The air was as still and cold as death, and the fog was a smothering blanket.

They had made love again that evening despite the discovery of Mitchell's body. Losing themselves in each other was their only release from all the troubles surrounding them.

Art Rekeby's death hadn't been a cause for celebration. It had been a shock from which the townsfolk would require time to recover. Their innocence had been lost and they were only now starting to understand that they had been manipulated with surprising ease. It was going to take a long time for them to regain faith in themselves.

All the same, several residents had already taken the covers off their letterboxes and mail slots, determined to make life go back to normal, even though George hadn't yet returned to delivering mail. Nobody would ever be able to check for mail the way they had before. The simple act of lifting the letterbox lid and looking inside had now become a daunting ritual. There would always be the underlying fear that they would find something so disturbing it would send them spiralling out of control, an object, letter, or image that would touch a raw nerve.

Ian watched Charlotte smoke, each ghostly plume escaping her lips to flee through the window and join the fog outside. It was a filthy habit, but he supposed he could put up with it on special occasions. He recalled the cigarette he'd found in the churchyard. It was still in his possession, the one clue he trusted. He thought about the brand name printed around it, just above the filter.

'Ian,' Charlotte whispered urgently, her head suddenly

enshrouded in smoke. 'Look!'

He leaped from his bed and joined her at the window. Through the foggy streetscape, they could vaguely distinguish a form, apparently human. It was barely moving, just standing there, standing in front of Ian's letterbox, and removing the plastic cover.

'The Postman!' Ian wanted to scream, but forced himself to release no more than a hiss from his mouth.

He didn't even take the time to pull his trousers back on, nor to tell Charlotte to stay inside and call Sergeant Manning. All he did was grab the cricket bat from under his bed and get outside as quickly as possible. The idea of finally confronting the Postman and the shot of adrenaline pumping through his almost naked body were stronger than his fear.

He ripped the front door open so violently it seemed it might come off its hinges and rushed outside.

The Postman was covered in his long black raincoat and hidden in the fog, but he turned and for a brief moment and Ian glimpsed his face. It wasn't enough to let him see who it was, to confirm what he suspected.

Ian clutched his bat with both hands and glanced at the window where Charlotte was hidden. He could see only the faint glow of her cigarette.

The Postman wouldn't simply vanish this time. He no longer had his bicycle, having left it for the police to find at Art Rekeby's house. This was the end, one way or another. Charlotte was either about to witness the heroic capture of a dangerous maniac or the death of the man she loved, before even having the chance to tell him just how she felt.

Ian stood frozen, his feet gripping the cold ground, not really sure what he was going to do. He waited to see what kind of weapon the Postman would produce, expecting the spine-tingling glint of a long blade accompanied by a cruel smile from inside the Postman's hood, a blurry glimpse of a sharp death. But the Postman turned and ran, his black coat sailing away into the fog.

He was almost as fast on his feet as he'd been on his bicycle, and Ian's fear for his life was replaced with the dreadful possibility that once more the Postman would get away.

He launched himself down the street in pursuit, heading towards the old cemetery. Despite wearing only a pair of boxers, he wasn't cold. The blood pumping through him was hot with determination and anger. The mild-mannered school teacher had become a primitive hunter, reduced to man at his most basic level.

The Postman came in and out of Ian's field of vision as they ran. The fog was taunting him, concealing and exposing incessantly. A matter of seconds was all that separated capture from escape. One moment, Ian could see the black form in front of him, seeming to glide like a giant bat rather than run, and the next it was swallowed by the fog.

Ian kept running, pushing himself, wondering if he would be able to keep up. Ignoring the pain that was building in his legs, he chased the Postman past the cemetery, where the campaign of terror had begun, and before long they were out of town.

The Postman's pace slowed and Ian tried to catch up with him, but his legs had wearied as well. The chase continued, the Postman never looking back.

Although Ian couldn't clearly see where they were, he knew they were approaching the moors. It was an area he didn't know well, another world where he would be lost, in flat fields and maze-like paths that wound around rocky outcrops and treacherous quagmires.

If the Postman left the road and knew where he was going, Ian would be at his mercy.

He did just that, veering to the left, staggering like a wounded animal, no longer gliding.

Ian found himself faced with a vital decision, whether to enter the unknown territory of the moors or abandon the chase. But his legs led him to the left, off the road and onto wet ground. They had chosen for him. There was no turning back.

The surface was uneven, alternating between swampy holes and slippery rocks. Ian nearly tripped over several times, and asked himself whether he would be able to get up again if he fell.

He imagined himself squirming on the ground, his cricket bat held by an arm too weak to lift it, the Postman looming over him, his face finally exposed as he tore Ian apart.

'Where are you?' Ian tried to shout, addressing his foe for the first time. But he immediately regretted his stupidity. The feigned bravado came out as a pitifully breathless cry of desperation.

There was no reply. Nothing but silence and darkness.

He'd lost sight of the Postman.

He stumbled through the fog, not really knowing where he was going, and nearly fell into a quagmire.

To one side was a pile of rocks, the height of a man, so he climbed up them, ignoring the pain in his feet. He hoped he would be able to spot the Postman from the top of the craggy outcrop.

He looked around, into the darkness of the moor, into the unknown, then he came tumbling down, his body bashing against jagged rocks. But lying on the cold ground, only one thought troubled him. He hadn't slipped. He'd been pulled down. Ian had distinctly felt a hand pull at his ankle.

He'd lost his breath in the fall and his head had hit the ground hard. He wanted to get to his feet, to find the Postman, but the gloved hand pushing against his chest told him searching was unnecessary.

The Postman loomed over him, his face still hooded. There was a thick chain slung across one shoulder, and Ian wondered what it was for. What was the maniac going to do to him?

'Ian, Ian, Ian.' It was the voice of a man with no remorse, as deep and empty as an abandoned mineshaft.

'You know my name?' Ian rasped painfully, pretending he hadn't already deduced the Postman's identity.

The Postman pulled his hood back and showed his face, and at that moment, Ian knew he was going to die, that his corpse would be left to rot on the moor, or even worse, be cut up and delivered to letterboxes and mail slots all around Mirebury.

'I know everybody's name,' he replied, then smiled chillingly. 'But you knew it was me, didn't you? There wasn't a hint of surprise on your face just now. How did you know?'

'The cigarette you left in the churchyard when you followed me on patrol. I've only seen two people in town smoking that brand.'

'Is that a fact? I only smoke Marlboro Reds. The other person must be Harry.'

'I figured it had to be one of you. I know Harry pretty well, enough to know he's a decent fellow. On the other hand, you've always struck me as being a bit unhinged.'

'Unhinged, am I? What a lovely compliment. Thank you so much. I have to admit I'm a little disappointed in you, Ian. You're not as sharp as I'd thought. You were Mirebury's only hope. That's why I chose you. I concede the cigarette was a spot of carelessness on my part, but I placed a set of clues in your hands from the very beginning. If only you'd picked up on that, you could have prevented all this. You could have saved three lives. It's not all my fault. You share the blame. I gave you a sporting chance.'

'What are you talking about?'

'I know you help Mary Hopkins with her crosswords when they get a bit too tricky for the poor old dear. Did you know you can create your own and submit them to newspapers?'

Ian was speechless.

'Do you remember the last crossword before my experiment began?'

'I think so.' He tried to remember.

'Didn't you find my name?'

'Your name was in the crossword?'

'You're disappointing me, Ian. You're spoiling my fun.'

'I'm trying.'

Ian's mind raced. He thought back to that last crossword. It was coming back to him.

'Try harder, teacher!'

'Yes,' Ian gasped, remembering. '*Hart. A beast of venery.*'

'There you go! I knew she'd need a helping hand with that clue. It was my crossword, and every solution was a clue. They have all

167

come to pass now. It's too late. All but one, that is.'

Which one? Ian tried to remember the crossword in its entirety, but he couldn't.

'What were you going to put in my letterbox?'

'Going to put?' He laughed. 'I *did* put something in your letterbox, and I suspect that by now Charlotte has made the rather unfortunate mistake of looking inside. You spoiled my experiment by coming up with the idea of putting the town's letterboxes out of commission. What did you expect me to do? Did you think I'd just throw in the towel and go back to business as usual, pottering around with beer pumps and bad wiring?' he asked bitterly. 'You've ruined years of preparation. You chose to end my game, Ian. This is how it ends. I win.'

Ian tried to get up, but Aiden's hand was strong and held him down.

'*At the sharp end of fashion.* That's the remaining word,' Aiden reminded him.

Ian recalled the answer, and its original meaning. He struggled, trying to roll free, but his attempts were futile.

Aiden's other hand had been hidden behind his back, but he now raised it above his head. Clasped in the black glove was a stiletto, the thin dagger favoured by mediaeval assassins.

'I can tell you're wondering what she found in your letterbox and what the consequences of that discovery will be.'

Aiden grinned mockingly.

'The thing is, Ian, *you will never know.*'

The dagger came stabbing down, aimed at Ian's heart, but he struggled with enough determination to put Aiden slightly off balance. The blade sank into his shoulder and he cried out, his howl booming across the moor.

Aiden leaned down and put his lips to Ian's ear.

'I have a confession to make. I've not yet had the honour of killing a fellow human. Not with my own hands anyway. You'll have to forgive me if I'm not very good at murder.'

'I can't pretend to appreciate the difficulties you've had,' Ian groaned, desperately vying for time. 'I can't fix whatever's broken inside you. But your little brother looks up to you. I thought you were his rock, but you've been poisoning his mind, haven't you? You want him to be just like you.'

'I want him to be strong. I want him to be a survivor.'

Ian wanted to tell him that he was Owen's worst enemy, but it would have been a fatal mistake. He had to keep Aiden talking.

'Why are you doing this? Why do you hate Mirebury?'

'Don't try to psychoanalyse me. My mind functions on a whole different level. If you crawl in there, you'll never find your way out again.'

'I just want to know why.'

'It's not that I hate Mirebury. I hate mankind. This town just happened to be mine, and the perfect setting for my letterbox experiment.'

'It's as simple as that?'

'It's a simple as that. Now, let's cut the conversation, if you please.'

He straightened himself up and pulled the dagger out.

The pain made Ian growl.

'I'm sorry, my good man. Did that hurt? Not to worry. The pain will be all over soon.'

Anger raged within Ian's blurry consciousness as the gloved hand raised the blade high above Aiden's head. Drops of blood fell onto Ian's face. Aiden was smiling, and taking his time, trying to make the thrill of the kill last as long as possible.

Ian's attention was fixed on the thin blade and the horrible drops of blood falling from it. The next stab would be more effective. He had to act quickly. An image of Charlotte flashed through his mind. He wanted to be with her, to hold her and never let go. He didn't want her to lay flowers on his coffin while Father Godfrey blabbered on about what a great teacher and friend he'd been and how the mild-mannered scholar would be sorely missed by Mirebury.

Ian snarled. He wouldn't let this monster win. He despised him. He was *better* than him. Behind his gentle appearance, there was a beast all of his own, and it was savage beyond reckoning.

Ian still had his cricket bat lying in the palm of his tired right hand. He gripped it, feeling his fingers tighten around it as best they could, and with a grunt, he swung with the little force he could muster.

The blow wasn't hard but it hit Aiden's jaw and made him jump backwards, wiping the smile off his face.

Ian struggled to his feet, not looking at the blood that covered his chest, and blocking out the burning pain in his shoulder.

Aiden had stumbled so far back that he'd almost vanished from Ian's field of vision again.

He lunged at him, swinging again, harder this time. But he missed. The dark form dropped back into the fog, so he staggered forward, ready to strike out again.

But Aiden wasn't there. The chain that had been slung across his shoulder was lying on the ground, eerily inoffensive in the fog.

Ian looked all about and found his opponent below him.

He'd fallen into a quagmire and was struggling to get out, but his thrashing was having the opposite effect. He was being devoured by the unforgiving moor. He was already waist deep in the treacherous earth, with his long coat floating around him, making it appear that he was melting, not sinking.

Before long, he stopped trying to work his way out. Resistance was futile. His gloved hands reached out for a lifeline. The cold blue eyes had lost their menace and now pleaded like those of a frightened child.

'I'm sinking, Ian. You have to help me. *Please.*'

Ian approached the edge of the pit. He had to be careful not to fall into the quagmire himself.

'I'm going under.'

'I thought you hated mankind? You hate me, don't you? Why would I help you after what you've put Mirebury through?'

Ian knelt down at the edge. His entire body was shaking and fatigued. His brain was confused and vague.

'You can't leave me here. It's not right. Owen needs me.'

'Owen needs you? How deluded you are!'

Ian hesitated. His mind was ticking over, trying to decide what to do.

'You're a good man, Ian. You're a man of honour.'

The cricket bat in his right hand was so heavy Ian thought his arm would be torn from his battered body.

Aiden's arms were outstretched. He was begging for his life. It was both pathetic and heart-breaking.

'You believe in humanity, Ian. You don't know how lucky you are to have that. You're a good man.'

Ian's mind stopped ticking over. There was only one option, after all. He had to do the right thing. He leaned over the unreliable edge of the quagmire, the cricket bat held out.

Aiden breathed a sigh of relief and clutched at the end of the bat, accepting Ian's mercy. A wicked smile formed on his lips, but it faded an instant later as Ian brought the bat back and lifted it as high as he could over his head.

It was not mercy he was offering, but deliverance.

The bat came crashing down, and the crack of willow on bone boomed across the moors like thunder.

Ian struck several times, and Aiden's body slumped, his battered head hanging uselessly. He then lowered the gore covered bat to Aiden's chest, balancing at the edge of the quagmire as he did so, and pushed.

The body sank deeper.

He kept pushing until no trace of the Postman remained, until he had been completely swallowed by the unforgiving moor.

Ian was alone, more alone than he'd ever been; exposed yet somehow embraced by the moors.

It took him a moment to come to terms with what he'd just done, but the pain in his shoulder and the bleeding wound stopped him from dwelling on it too long. He took his boxers off and used them to apply pressure. The dagger had gone deep and he'd already lost a great deal of blood.

As he stumbled back to the road, he thought about Charlotte and realised how much he cared for her. He was alive for her and wanted to spend the life he had almost lost with her.

Aiden's words echoed in his head.

I did put something in your letterbox, *and I suspect that by now Charlotte has made the rather unfortunate mistake of looking inside.*

He stumbled along the road, his naked body aching, and his shoulder still bleeding despite his attempt to keep his boxers pressed hard against the wound. His letterbox filled his mind and helped him ignore the pain. He had to get home before she decided to look inside it. He couldn't bear the thought of anything happening to her.

31

Blue lights flashed through the thick fog. There was no way of telling where they were coming from because the tiny particles of moisture in the air reflected the light. Ian was surrounded by the pulsating glow. He knew immediately that Charlotte had called Sergeant Manning. There was no blaring siren to accompany the light, and for an instant, Ian wondered whether his hearing was failing him. But he quickly realised the reason. Traffic in Mirebury was always light during the day and generally inexistent at night. He was sure the sergeant had decided to leave the siren off to avoid causing further panic, warning the whole town that trouble was afoot.

The time it had taken the sergeant to react seemed odd to Ian. Why so long? Or perhaps Charlotte had got flustered and hesitated to make the call. Then it dawned on him that neither of those factors came into play. The combat hadn't lasted as long as Ian felt it had. That's all there was to it. It had felt like a drawn-out ordeal to him, but in fact had probably only lasted a few minutes.

None of that mattered now. What was important was that it was all over. He felt immeasurably relieved. His knees were growing weak and his body seemed strangely light and heavy at the same time, giving the absurd impression that the likelihood of collapsing in a pile was no greater than that of floating away into the fog.

The Range Rover drew nearer and Ian could see the source of the blue lights more clearly. He stumbled away from the middle of the road so he wouldn't get run over as the vehicle shot out of the fog. Sergeant Manning applied the brakes and brought it to a screeching halt.

'Ian!'

'Here, Simon!'

'Bloody hell! You're stark naked. You must be freezing!'

The sergeant opened the boot of his vehicle and removed a thermal blanket.

'Being naked is the least of my worries.'

Sergeant Manning gently wrapped the blanket around Ian.

'Art wasn't the Postman after all!'

'No, he wasn't.'

'I'm such an idiot.'

He led Ian to the Range Rover and helped him inside.

'That's a nasty wound you've got there, Ian. We'll get that fixed up right away,' he said, already calling Gordon. The doctor was presumably asleep, but he eventually picked up. The sergeant gave him a brief of the situation and the nature of Ian's injury as he hurried around the front of the vehicle and got in behind the wheel. He hung up and looked across at Ian, his face beaming with admiration.

'Let's get you to Gordon and find out how bad that shoulder really is.'

He pumped the accelerator and spun the Range Rover around.

'We have to go to my place first, Simon.'

'I'm afraid that's out of the question. You need to get that shoulder fixed up immediately.'

'You don't understand. I think there might be something dangerous in my letterbox. I don't want Charlotte to open it.'

The sergeant grinned briefly.

'The librarian's staying at your place, you cheeky devil? You two didn't waste any time.'

Ian tried to smile, but could only groan.

'I have to check the letterbox!'

'All right. Calm down. It's on the way to Gordon's place.'

Simon stared into the fog in front of him as they passed the cemetery.

'Ian?'

'Yes.'

'So, who *is* the Postman?'

'It was Aiden.'

Simon gasped.

'I've never liked him but he's never given me any major trouble before. Wait a minute! Why did you say *was*?'

Ian turned to him.

'There was an incident, involving a quagmire. Can we talk about that later?'

The sergeant nodded slowly.

'He fell into a quagmire. You tried to help him out but couldn't reach him. He went under and you stumbled back to the road. You don't know where any of it happened. You were lost, confused, and losing blood.'

Ian nodded. 'That's exactly what happened.'

'Good.'

He stopped the Range Rover in front of Ian's house. Through the fog, behind the curtains, the lights were on and glowing defiantly. Across the street, Mrs Hopkins and her daughter were watching from the window. Poor Mrs Hopkins must have been terrified for Ian. He thought about going over to reassure her that he was still alive and that everybody in Mirebury would be safe from now on, but he decided there would be time for that later.

'Stay here and keep pressure on your shoulder.'

Simon jumped out and strode over to Ian's letterbox, but an anxious voice interrupted him.

'Sergeant! Hello, sergeant!'

Charlotte came out, dressed in a warm nightdress.

'Is Ian in there?'

'Yes.'

'Thank goodness. Is he all right?'

'He'll be fine, but he needs medical attention. Jump in the Range Rover if you like. We're going to the doctor's house as soon as I've checked Ian's letterbox.'

She rushed over to the passenger door.

'Ian!' She put a hand on his weary head. 'Tell me what happened. Who's the Postman? Where is he now?'

Ian looked into her loving eyes.

'I promise I'll tell you everything, but not right now.'

She wiped blood from his face and then kissed him on the forehead. The idea that she may have lost him melted away as her lips touched his cold skin. Her mind and body, after what had seemed like hours of tension, relaxed a little.

Simon called out from where he stood beside Ian's letterbox.

'Ian, there's nothing in here. It's empty.'

'Did you check the letterbox after I left?' he asked her.

'Are you joking? I didn't leave the house. I locked the doors, called Sergeant Manning, and waited at your bedroom window, begging I would see you alive and well again.'

'It's strange, don't you think? Didn't we see him remove the plastic cover and put something in the letterbox?'

Charlotte frowned, trying to remember the terrible moment she noticed the foggy form standing outside Ian's house.

'Yes, we saw him at the letterbox, but I don't recall actually seeing him place anything inside. Is it important?'

Ian shook his head slowly. He wasn't sure whether it was important or not, but it didn't make sense, and his teacher's instinct always drove him to try to understand the misunderstood.

'What was he doing at my house if he wasn't making a delivery?'

Charlotte didn't know what to say. He was right. What *did* it mean?

'Sergeant,' Charlotte called out. 'Are you absolutely *sure* there's nothing in the letterbox?'

'Yes, quite sure.'

'Was the plastic cover on it?' she asked.

'No, it's on the ground... hold on...'

'What is it?' Ian asked with a strained voice.

'There's something on the ground here!'

'Well? What is it, sergeant?'

'I don't really know. I'll show you.'

Simon came over to them and handed a small plastic object to Charlotte. She held it in front of Ian so he could see what it was.

The tiny letterbox was a scale model of Ian's, exact in every detail. Even the scratches on the paintwork had been copied. It was covered in a plastic cover just like those that George had wrapped over every letterbox in town according to Ian's plan.

'He was angry at me for having dared to prevent him from making his deliveries.'

Charlotte lifted the letterbox up to her face so she could see it more clearly. She looked across to Ian's letterbox, floating innocently in the fog.

The resemblance was disturbing.

'Let's go now,' the sergeant said, getting behind the wheel.

Charlotte climbed in beside Ian.

The Range Rover faded into the fog.

'Look, Ian. I can take the plastic off it.'

He watched as she removed the cover.

'I'm not sure you should.'

'You think it'll explode?'

But she didn't wait for him to reply. She slowly lifted the lid off the letterbox and peered inside.

'The sick maniac!'

'What's in there?'

She held it out to him and he looked inside. There were three tiny figurines. They were in a landscape that was unmistakable; the moors. One was a hooded form with a naked woman kneeling at his feet. He held one end of a chain in his hands. The other end was wrapped around the woman's neck. In front of them, lying amidst rocks and quagmires, was Ian. A dagger was planted in his chest.

He shivered.

'He had it all planned. He knew I would follow him into the moors. He was going to stab me to death out there. He very nearly did. Then he was going to come back for you, Charlotte. He had a chain on him. I wondered why at the time. He was going to strip you off, chain you up, and drag you to my corpse. Then...'

'Stop it, Ian! That's enough.'

She felt sick inside.

'Maybe he had it all planned, Ian, but he got it wrong.'

She took his hand away from his shoulder and held his boxers against the wound for him.

'He counted on you following him into the moors, but he didn't count on you being the one to walk back out.'

32

Doctor Sykes was waiting for them on the doorstep.

'Come inside quickly,' he told the three of them. 'It would be best to avoid too much commotion if we can, until I've attended to the patient and you've put me in the picture.'

They followed him inside, Sergeant Manning close behind the doctor, Ian pressing his boxers against the wound, and Charlotte quietly closing the front door behind them. The chances of them having arrived unnoticed were slim, especially with everyone so nervously peering out from behind curtains these days. They would know soon enough. Mrs Hopkins wouldn't call anyone in the middle of the night, knowing that Sergeant Manning had the situation under control, but there were plenty of looser tongues in town, and fingers that wouldn't hesitate to dial numbers in the dead of night if there was gossip and conjecture to be spread.

Helen whispered a greeting to them, unable to hide the look of concern on her face, and continued preparing a pot of tea. The children were still in bed. Unusual as it was for the doctor to have an emergency of this nature in the middle of the night, he knew how to react quickly and discreetly.

'Sit here, Ian,' the doctor said, indicating a straight-backed chair. 'Keep your arms down by your side,' he instructed, taking the boxers from his patient's hand. His tone was comforting and his gaze keen and analytical.

'How bad is it?' Charlotte asked, her voice strained.

'The bleeding has slowed. His heart is still in one piece,' the doctor reassured her, winking. 'I'd recommend you go easy on it for a few weeks all the same.'

'I think I can manage that.'

'You'll be fine, young man. A bit of a clean and a stitch job is all that's in order tonight. You'll just need to come back to show me how it looks in a couple of days. Mind you, it was a matter of half an inch. Best avoid getting into knife fights in the future in my humble medical opinion. I don't think it's quite your thing. How's the other fellow?' Doctor Sykes narrowed his eyes.

'Beyond your talents, Gordon,' the sergeant said. 'Ian did his best but couldn't save him.'

The doctor raised his eyebrows and went about preparing to stitch his patient up. 'You mentioned a quagmire on the phone, Simon.'

'Ian doesn't know where they were. He chased him from outside his house, up past the cemetery.'

'Past the cemetery and left or right of the road?'

Ian and Simon shared a cautious glance, but it failed to go unnoticed.

'Come along now. I may be a doctor, but that doesn't mean my goodwill and forgiveness is limitless, despite whatever you may have heard. A monster capable of inflicting a wound like this on a chap like Ian, not to mention all the torment the town has gone through, deserves not an ounce of pity.'

'He turned left,' Ian admitted. 'It's hard to judge the distance after the cemetery.'

'Roughly three quarters of a mile?'

Ian's eyes widened. 'That sounds about right.'

'There was a craggy mound, about six feet high, and a deep quagmire the size of a fishpond a few feet behind it?'

'That's exactly what it was like,' Ian replied, looking away from his shoulder as the doctor began stitching.

'He couldn't have picked a better spot,' the doctor mused, a certain hint of admiration in his voice. 'He sank?'

Ian looked at Simon again, but neither of them uttered a word.

The doctor smiled. 'It's over then. I know the moors, and I know that part of it. He'll not been seen again. Keep your lips sealed. Maintain that you were so scared and confused you don't even remember which way you went from outside your house. I'll vouch for your state of mind.'

Ian nodded. 'Thank you.'

'No,' the doctor reprimanded him. 'Thank *you*, Ian. We all owe you a debt of gratitude that we'll never really be able to declare appropriately. As far as I'm concerned, and I'm sure the same goes for the whole town, what you did was right. It was the only way. Unfortunately, the wheels of justice don't only turn slowly, they often turn the wrong way. It's a risk you can't afford to take. It stays between us.'

Helen came in with the teapot and cups. 'Not a word. I may be inclined to gossip when it comes to budding romance, but I know how to keep a secret. Believe me.'

Gordon finished dressing Ian's wound, and looked him straight in the eye. 'It was one of us?'

'Simon didn't tell you?' Ian asked, turning to the sergeant.

The doctor shook his head. 'Don't tell me it was Damian?'

Ian laughed, but the pain made him stop.

'Why do you say that?' the sergeant asked.

'I don't know. No reason. Who else could it be?'

'Aiden Hart.'

The doctor nodded slowly, then a dark frown covered his face.

'Aiden,' he said. 'I suppose I should have guessed. The poor lad never had a chance, between his parents and Cherry Somers. Perhaps I could have helped him. I suggested a counsellor once, but he never came to see me again after that.'

'Believe me, Gordon. He was beyond help.'

'What happens now?' Charlotte asked.

'There will be an intrusive investigation by CID. The five of us will stay tight-lipped, corroborate Ian's version of the events, and everybody will support him,' the sergeant said.

'Are you up to it, Ian?' the doctor asked.

'I think I am. I have to be.'

'You've already overcome your greatest fear and achieved one of your main goals in life tonight, Ian,' Charlotte said. 'That's pretty impressive.'

'I haven't the faintest idea what you mean.'

'You've barely even noticed you were naked in public, and you certainly got closer to nature.'

He tried not to laugh. He really tried.

'It's about time we made you decent,' Gordon said. 'Helen, can you fetch the poor lad some clothes? Have I still got that old tracksuit tucked away in a vacuum bag in the wardrobe? The one with blood stains that I keep for doing odd jobs.' He looked at Ian and shrugged. 'You're not the only one to go for a jog in the moors and come back the worse for wear.'

33

When life in Mirebury would return to normal was hard to say, but with the Postman gone, the dark clouds were already beginning to disperse. The search for Aiden's body was proving fruitless and the investigation seemed destined to slow down to the point of bureaucratic symbolism.

The CID unit had failed to secure any evidence indicating who had murdered Art Rekeby. Mitchell Somers remained their prime suspect, but he'd left no clue whatsoever as to the identity of his accomplices. The fact that no witnesses had come forward further complicated matters. The inspector could feel the case growing colder with each passing hour. He consulted Sergeant Manning and Doctor Sykes on the matter of Ian's character and state of mind, and he took their statements regarding the events immediately prior to and following the duel.

Aiden's workshop was searched and confirmation of his meticulously conceived game was found. There were detailed files about most of the town's inhabitants on his laptop, along with digitally altered photographs of Cherry and Brett. There was a padlocked metal trunk under his workbench, and inside was a pile of broken gadgets, old batteries and cables, as well as the charred remains of a newspaper, enough of which remained to detect that letters had been cut out of certain words. At least that was conclusive.

But Mirebury was not yet done with strange happenings. Three nights after the Postman's demise, there was movement upon the moors. Five beams of torchlight danced through the nocturnal gloom and fog as a group of residents converged on the hollow that had been designated as their meeting place. It was on the opposite side of town from where the fatal confrontation with the Postman had taken place. This secluded spot, known to all but rarely frequented, was Foxglove Hollow. It was the very spot where just days earlier, unbeknownst to the group, Jenny Somers had met with the Postman.

The beams drew closer together until they united to form a single sphere of bright light. The faces of those who had come became clearer. They formed a tight circle inside the hollow, making sure to stand on solid ground.

'We are all here.'

It was Mayor Larkins who had spoken.

'Thank you all for accepting to gather here tonight. I know it's extremely risky, but I think the alternative would have proved even riskier. We have all made a grave mistake.'

'That we have,' one of them agreed.

'I will not pretend that it's not my fault, for I was the fool who fell into the Postman's trap and dragged you down with me. I failed to tell you about the message I received in my letterbox just before Ian's idea was put into action. I regret that terribly because I know that if I'd told you, you would have convinced me to ignore it as just another manipulation. I've been a hypocrite, telling the good men and women of Mirebury not to fall for the Postman's ploys when I was the most gullible of all.'

'We made the mistake together, Edward. Each of us is as guilty as the others. It's a burden we must all carry. But why didn't you suspect the message had been written by the Postman?'

'It was sent to me by Jenny Somers. She told me she'd seen Art riding a bicycle that sounded like the one Ian and Jack had heard a few days earlier.'

'You're saying you didn't suspect it may have been a forgery, written by the Postman?'

'I most certainly did, and I called Jenny Somers myself. She confirmed that the letter was hers and that she had indeed seen the Postman's bicycle in Art's possession.'

'So, was she lying, or did Art simply steal the bicycle from the Postman somehow?'

'I suspect the first situation is the most likely because I can't imagine how anybody could have stolen the bicycle of a phantom that we couldn't even catch.'

'Mayor Larkins, what you're saying is that Jenny is responsible for having manipulated us in order to make us kill Art for her?'

The Mayor nodded his head solemnly.

'It's unbelievable. That's not Jenny Somers. She isn't the kind of woman to incite murder. I've never known her to be vindictive or calculating. What could her motive have been?'

'Surely you know all about what Cherry and Art had going on between them?'

'Yes, I see your point. She was far from fond of Art, that was common knowledge, but I didn't know she had it in her to arrange his murder.'

'I didn't know it either,' the mayor continued. 'It wasn't until I heard that Ian had confronted the real Postman that I realised Jenny had manipulated me.'

'That's beastly.'

'It certainly is, but I've tried to put myself in her shoes. I suppose she just wasn't thinking straight. Her husband had disappeared and I suspect the Postman blackmailed her, telling her that if she didn't do as she was told, she would never see him alive again.'

'That's plausible. But even if the Postman had intended to keep his word, he couldn't have prevented Mitchell from taking his own life.'

'At any rate, we can't expose Jenny,' somebody pointed out. 'If she were held responsible for what she did, we would also find ourselves behind bars.'

'That's right. We're in this together with Jenny, even though she probably doesn't know about the rest of you,' the mayor said.

'As long as we all keep quiet, we'll be fine.'

'Yes, and that's exactly why it was necessary for me to ask you to leave your comfortable homes and come to this hidden hollow tonight.'

'I'm not sure,' John Phelps admitted. 'Was it necessary?'

'I believe so,' Mayor Larkins continued. 'We've been very

careful so far and succeeded in covering our tracks. There's just one item of damning evidence to be disposed of, and we ought to do that together so we all know it has been destroyed.'

'The letter?' John asked. 'You still have it?'

'I've kept it locked away in the council safe, but I've brought it here tonight.'

The others watched as he removed it from his coat, along with a small rectangular object. A lighter. Their faces glowed as the letter burned, and relief flickered in their eyes. The fire completely consumed the letter, and the mayor sucked his fingertips as the last smouldering ash drifted to the damp ground at his feet.

'It's important we make a promise to each other. What was the word you used, Father Godfrey?'

'A covenant, Edward.'

'We need to make a covenant. We must swear we'll never speak about our mistake to anybody else—ever.'

The six residents of Mirebury hummed in agreement. It was a promise they were eager to make.

'Let us forgive each other if we can find it in ourselves to do so,' Father Godfrey suggested solemnly. 'Let us pray night and day that the Lord will pardon us for our foolishness and sinful behaviour. He will do as He sees fit.'

Mayor Larkins placed his right hand in the middle of the circle, where the beams of their torches met.

Doctor Sykes put his right hand, usually dedicated to healing, onto Mayor Larkins's. That fateful night, the very same hand had thrust a pitchfork through Art's neck.

John Phelps added his right hand, usually dedicated to burying the dead, not pinning the living against bedroom walls.

Vernon White's right hand, the soft hand of a bank manager, came forward. It had been capable of work harder and dirtier than it was used to doing.

Father Godfrey, whose hands were usually clasped together in prayer, offered his right hand. All the prayers in the world could not undo the evil work they had been put to. While he'd been preaching to his flock about the influence of evil, it had crept up behind him and caught him off guard.

Dear old Mary Hopkins had been a witness to the gruesome murder. Her participation had not been physical, but she was as guilty as the others because she'd made no attempt to stop them. When Vernon had told her about the mayor's discovery, she'd come out of hiding. She'd known full well they weren't planning on turning him over to Sergeant Manning. While the men had dispensed bloody justice on her tormentor, she'd thought about her husband's disturbed remains.

She placed her right hand on top of the others.

'Repeat after me,' Mayor Larkins said. 'We promise to keep our mistake a secret for ever. We will never speak of Art Rekeby's murder to anyone, not even to each other.'

They repeated his words slowly, and in unison, with solemn voices.

'Let us now go back to our homes and put this behind us for good,' Mayor Larkins said, ushering them in the direction of the narrow gap leading out of the hollow.

They turned and walked away, up through the crags and into the fog, going their separate ways. All except for Vernon and Mary, who left together. He held a torch in one hand and guided Mary with the other. He would take her back to her house where her daughter was waiting for her to come back from their game of Scrabble.

The beams of light drifted away into the fog, moving this way and that as the treacherous ground was negotiated. The night reclaimed the moor, enshrouding it in timeless mystery.

The Postman's Crossword

Across

3. To distort the reality of images
7. Yorick's body part
9. Acquired through study and practice
10. Red sweetness wrapped around a stone
11. A provider of intimacy
12. Painted to appear guilty
13. Beast of venery

Down

1. A human in your vicinity
2. Old English food
4. At the sharp end of fashion
5. One bankrupt in a vegan world
6. Treacherous land
8. A transmitter of knowledge
11. Eight-legged or spouseless

ANSWERS ON THE NEXT PAGE

Across
3. photoshop
7. skull
9. art
10. cherry
11. whore
12. framed
13. hart

Down
1. neighbour
2. meat
4. stiletto
5. butcher
6. quagmire
8. teacher
11. widow

**BLACK
BEACON
B O O K S**

blackbeaconbooks.com